THE DEMON HEADMASTER

MORTAL DANGER

The most hypnotic villain of all . . .

Get ready for adventure and intrigue.

Prepare to fall under his spell.

Do not try to resist . . .

KT-559-537

OXFORD
UNIVERSITY PRESS

Great Clarendon Street, Oxford OX2 6DP

Oxford University Press is a department of the University of Oxford.
It furthers the University's objective of excellence in research, scholarship,
and education by publishing worldwide. Oxford is a registered trade mark
of Oxford University Press in the UK and in certain other countries

Copyright © Gillian Cross 2019
Character illustration © Robin Boyden 2019

The moral rights of the author have been asserted

Database right Oxford University Press (maker)

First published 2019

All rights reserved. No part of this publication may be reproduced,
stored in a retrieval system, or transmitted, in any form or by any means,
without the prior permission in writing of Oxford University Press,
or as expressly permitted by law, or under terms agreed with the appropriate
reprographics rights organization. Enquiries concerning reproduction
outside the scope of the above should be sent to the Rights Department,
Oxford University Press, at the address above

You must not circulate this book in any other binding or cover
and you must impose this same condition on any acquirer

British Library Cataloguing in Publication Data

Data available

ISBN: 978-0-19-276606-9

1 3 5 7 9 10 8 6 4 2

Printed in Great Britain

Paper used in the production of this book is a natural,
recyclable product made from wood grown in sustainable forests.
The manufacturing process conforms to the environmental
regulations of the country of origin.

GILLIAN CROSS

THE DEMON HEAD MASTER

MORTAL DANGER

OXFORD
UNIVERSITY PRESS

CONTENTS

1

MS MOUNTAIN

It was the new Head's first day at Hazelbrook Academy—
and no one had any idea what was just about to hit them.
As Lizzie walked into assembly, she saw Blake yawning
and looking at his watch.

'I bet she'll make a long, boring speech,' he said.
'Telling us lots of stuff we already know.'

'Well, she's not here yet,' Ethan said, as they
shuffled along the row. The stage was empty, except for
the lectern on one side and the screen at the back.

There was more shuffling and whispering as other
people came in and sat down. Then *Ssh! Ssh!* from the
teachers. And then silence.

But only for a split second. Then the door at the back
of the hall banged open and a woman came bounding
down the middle. Jumping onto the stage, she turned
to face them all.

Lizzie stared up at her in amazement. Was this the
new Head? She was *massive*. Tall and muscular, with a
huge halo of brown curls and glasses the size of dinner
plates.

Her grin was massive too, as she beamed down at
them all. 'Hello! I'm Ms Martin.'

'Ms *Mountain*!' said Blake.

It was meant to be a whisper, but dozens of people heard him, and there was a quick, scared gasp. You couldn't make jokes about the *Head*. Last term, that would have meant a terrifying trip to the Headmaster's office. And the sound of his cold voice saying, *Look into my eyes*.

No one ever remembered what happened after that, but thinking about it made them shiver . . .

So what would this new Head do? Lizzie felt the question hanging in the air. Even the teachers looked anxious. Mr Wasu's eyes were very wide open and Miss Wellington had a hand over her mouth. Was this term going to be another disaster?

Ms Martin stared back at them for a second, looking baffled. Then she threw her head back and roared with laughter.

'Don't look so *scared*! It takes more than a joke to upset *me*.' She gave them a huge grin. 'Call me whatever you like—as long as you're enjoying yourselves. That's the important thing. You'll learn much better if you're having fun.'

Fun? Lizzie blinked. *That* would be a change. Last term, the Headmaster had made her write a long, dull essay about Shakespeare's grammar. Things were obviously going to be different with Ms Martin in charge.

The new Head beamed down at them all. 'We're going to have a great term. And it's starting with a HUGE event! I know you'll love it. I just need to fix a few details with the other schools round here. Then I'll make an announcement. Did you see the new screen outside the hall? Keep an eye on that—and start thinking about what you *really like doing!*'

She grinned again and then jumped off the stage and ran down the hall. For a second, after the door banged behind her, there was utter silence. Then everyone started talking at once. And the teachers were just as excited as everyone else. As Lizzie went out of the hall she saw Mr Wasu grinning at Mrs Maron, the Deputy Head.

'Looks like being an amazing term!' he said.

The announcement appeared on the new screen at lunchtime—just as everyone was heading down to the canteen. The whole school came to a standstill. People crowded together outside the hall, staring up at the huge, glittering letters.

ARTS EXPLOSION!
SATURDAY 20TH APRIL
TWENTY SCHOOLS!! OVER TEN THOUSAND PEOPLE!!!
ALMOST AS BIG AS YOUR IMAGINATION!!*!!&&!!&@@!

Behind the headlines, pictures appeared and disappeared, one dissolving into another. Below that, smaller words scrolled up the screen:

DANCE SAMBA AND RUMBA AND ZUMBA

POETRY SLAM AND BRASS BAND JAM

SPRAY SOME GRAFFITI FOR TAHITI

WIN GLORY WITH A STORY

FIX COMPUTER GRAPHICS FROM NINE TO SIX

MAKE A PLAY IN A DAY—PAGE TO STAGE

RECORD-BREAKING BAKING—

The list went on and on.

Ethan shook his head, as if he could hardly believe it. '*Everything's* there! Music and drama and art and coding—'

'—and poetry and cooking—' Lizzie was excited too. 'And—'

'No, there *isn't* everything!' Lizzie's little brother Tyler bobbed up next to her, frowning crossly. 'There's no *magic* on that list.' He folded his arms and glared up at the screen.

Lizzie shook her head at him. 'Don't be silly, Ty. You can't have magic at school.'

'Why not?' boomed a voice from behind her. 'Having no magic is *tragic*!'

They whirled round—and there was the new Head, looming over them. She beamed at Tyler and opened her gigantic handbag.

'Don't worry, I'll fix it right now.' She pulled a tablet

out of the handbag—sending dozens of other things showering out along with it. Pens and notebooks and keys clattered on to the floor, and Lizzie and Ethan scrambled to pick them up.

Ms Martin didn't seem to notice. She was too busy tapping away at the tablet, so fast they could hardly see her fingers moving. After a few seconds, she stepped back and pointed up at the big screen.

'There you go. Now magic's on the menu too!'

And it was. She'd added another line to the scrolling words.

—TEST YOUR TRICKS IN THE MAGIC MIX
FROM NINE TO SIX—

'Yay!' shouted Tyler. 'Thanks, Ms Mountain!'

'Ty!' Lizzie elbowed him and looked up at the Head. 'I'm sorry, Ms Martin. He's just *really* excited. He's been doing magic tricks since he was five.'

'Don't *worry*.' The Head winked at Tyler. 'Good to have a magician in the school. I'd better go and find another one, to run the workshop.' She tossed the tablet into her bag and started walking away.

'Wait!' Ethan said. 'You dropped these.' He ran after her, with his hands full of things he'd picked up.

'And these!' Lizzie called, following him.

The Head beamed at them both, holding her bag wide open. 'Good work! Drop them in.' She squashed everything down on top of her tablet, and then headed off along the corridor, talking to everyone she passed.

Lizzie shook her head. 'She's like—like—'

'Like a Ferrari at full speed!' Ethan said.

Lizzie grinned. 'Like a rocket taking off into space!'

'Like a volcano erupting!' Ethan was laughing now. 'No wonder she's planning an Arts *Explosion*!'

They walked back towards the screen. 'It sounds great,' Lizzie said. 'But—can it really be that good?'

Tyler heard her, and he turned round and punched the air. 'Yesss! It's going to be amazing. Especially the magic workshop!'

'Especially the *band*!' That was Blake. 'I've always wanted to be a drummer!' He twirled a pair of imaginary drumsticks and started striding around, beating an invisible drum.

'Careful!' squealed Tyler. He leapt forward and snatched something off the ground. 'You nearly trod on this!'

Blake frowned at the DVD Tyler was waving in his face. 'What is it?'

Tyler peered at the cover. 'It says *To my—my*— something about success.'

'Let me see.' Lizzie held out her hand.

'It must be Ms Mountain's,' Ethan said, before Tyler could hand it over. 'Catch her before she goes into her office, Ty!'

Tyler shot away down the corridor and Lizzie shook her head at Ethan. 'Now *you're* doing it,' she said.

Ethan frowned. 'Doing what?'

'Calling her Ms Mountain. That's not her name.'

Blake laughed. 'It is now! Ms Mountain the Mighty!'

He marched off to the canteen, still playing his invisible drum.

Ethan looked back at the screen. 'The Arts Explosion is certainly going to be mighty,' he said. 'A computer graphics workshop! How great is that?'

'Not as great as the dance workshop!' said a voice behind him. It was Angelika—and she was grinning all over her face. 'I can't wait!'

All round them, people were shouting and laughing and looking excited. *I don't know what's on that 'to-my-success—' DVD*, Lizzie thought, *but it must be something special. Ms Mountain's going to be a SUPER-success!*

2

THE ARTS EXPLOSION

Ethan wasn't banging an imaginary drum, but he knew just how Blake felt. Because one of the Arts Explosion workshops was going to be about *computer graphics*. He'd just spent weeks building a new game, and the idea was sensational, but he knew the graphics let it down. If the Arts Explosion workshop was good, it would be exactly what he needed.

He couldn't wait.

And he didn't have to. Ms Mountain seemed to work at the speed of light. Less than two weeks after they first saw the announcement, Ethan woke up on Saturday morning and thought, *It's today! The Arts Explosion is TODAY!!*

He jumped out of bed and ran into the bathroom. Auntie Beryl must have heard him singing in the shower, because she was up before he'd finished. As he dressed, he could smell his breakfast cooking.

'You're up early,' she said, as she tossed the pancake.

'It's the Arts Explosion!' Ethan said. 'My workshop starts at nine o'clock.'

'Well you're not going without your breakfast,'

Auntie Beryl said. 'Bacon or sausages with your pancake?'

'Both!' Ethan said. '*And* a tomato, please. I'll need lots of energy today.'

He ate everything on his plate and then made himself a thick cheese sandwich. He packed it up with a banana and some of Auntie Beryl's fruit cake, and she beamed and patted his shoulder.

'I hope this *explosion* is going to be as good as you're hoping.'

Ethan put the lunchbox into his backpack. 'I'll tell you at teatime.'

Five minutes later he was on his bike, pedalling towards school as fast as he could go.

He nearly didn't make it. As he reached the last turn, there was a car coming in the opposite direction. He signalled left and started turning—but the car cut in front of him, swinging across the road without any warning.

Ethan stopped just in time. The car was a big, black Rolls Royce. It went by so close that he felt the wind as it passed and caught a quick flash of gold on its side. Its smoked windows hid the passenger in the back, but he saw the red-haired driver—who obviously had no idea he had nearly killed a cyclist. The car drove straight on down the road and turned in at the school entrance.

Ethan stood catching his breath for a moment. Then he set off for the school gates, as fast as he could. He was planning to find that driver—and tell him exactly what he thought of him!

But he hadn't really understood about the Arts Explosion.

He was expecting something like the school fête, with different workshops round the edge of the field and room to stroll around in the middle. So he could complain to the red-haired driver and then go and find his friends. Right?

Wrong! It wasn't like the fête *at all*.

It was more like a massive music festival, with hundreds of kids queuing to get in. There were stewards at the gates, handing out wristbands and checking people's bags, and teachers inside giving out programmes. They were all grinning and joking, as if they were on holiday, while more and more kids flooded past them. By the time Ethan reached the gate, the field, was so crowded he couldn't see across it.

It would be stupid to waste time looking for the black car. He padlocked his bike, collected his wristband and programme, and headed for the field, looking for Lizzie and the others.

But he hadn't gone far when he heard two voices shouting behind him.

'Ethan!'

'Hey, *Ethan*!'

He looked round and his mouth dropped open. 'Jatinder! Sam!' They were two of his best friends from his old school, before he came to Hazelbrook. What were they doing there?

They elbowed their way through to him and Jatinder

grabbed one of his arms. 'Don't hang about! It's starting in ten minutes!'

'Why . . . what . . .?' Ethan blinked at him.

'The computer graphics workshop, idiot.' Jatinder shook Ethan's arm with one of his big, strong hands. 'You *are* doing that one, aren't you?'

'Yes, of course,' Ethan said. 'But—'

'So we need to *hurry*.' Jatinder shook his head. 'It's booked solid. We need to get good seats.'

'OK.' Ethan grinned at Sam. 'Are you doing it too?'

'When there's a music workshop? Are you mad?' Sam shook his head. 'I'm going to write some new songs for the band!' He turned and started pushing his way through the crowd.

'So his band's still going?' Ethan said.

'Certainly is,' Jatinder grinned. 'They're getting really good. Sam's talking about getting some proper gigs.'

'That figures,' Ethan nodded. 'Sam's got a great voice.'

'And *we* are going to learn some great CGI stuff. Come on. The workshop's in the hall.' Jatinder hustled Ethan into the school building and the two of them pushed their way through the crowds in the corridor. Jatinder seemed to know the whole programme by heart. Including the map.

'The hall's up here, right?' He frowned as they turned the corner. 'Look at that queue! Hope there aren't any gate-crashers, or we might not get in.'

'It's OK.' Ethan saw a bright-red figure at the front

of the queue. It was Ms Mountain, in a scarlet dress, and she was checking off people's names as they went in. 'That's our new Head. Gate-crashers won't get past *her*.'

When they reached the front of the queue, Ms Mountain grinned and waved them through. 'Better grab a seat fast. It's starting in two minutes—and it's going to be grrrrreat!'

'Wow!' muttered Jatinder as they scrambled for seats together. 'She is *awesome*. She certainly beats Mr Ramsey.'

'Mr Ramsey's OK,' Ethan said. He liked the Head of his old school. 'Last term, when the Headmaster was here, I kept wishing we had Mr Ramsey instead. This school was—'

But there was no time to talk about the Headmaster and all the weird things that had happened last term. Because, just at that moment, two very young men came bounding through the hall. As they went by, Jatinder gasped.

'Look—it's *them*! Casey and Vijay. I can't believe it!'

He'd shouted it, at the top of his voice, and Vijay spun round and high-fived him as he passed. For a moment, Ethan thought Jatinder was going to faint with excitement.

Casey and Vijay were doing the workshop? Ethan stared as they reached the front and jumped onto the stage. He'd seen them online a thousand times, but he'd never thought—never dreamt—that ever, in a million years he would see them *live*. How had Ms Mountain fixed that?

There was a huge cheer as Casey and Vijay turned to face the audience. And then dead silence as the screen over the stage came to life. Everyone in the hall knew, straight away, what they were looking at.

It was a preview of the next version of **Scum Pirates**.

Casey beamed down at them all. 'So, let's show you how we create this stuff!'

3

THE WEIRD VOICE

Lizzie and Tyler were still waiting to get through the gate. Everyone was staring at them—because they'd brought Robo.

Tyler's robot.

'Are we supposed to give that thing an armband?' one of the stewards asked.

'He's not a *thing*!' Tyler said furiously. 'Don't talk about him like that, or he'll be upset. He's my *friend*.' He patted Robo's shoulder.

For an awful moment, Lizzie thought the men were going to laugh. But, just in time, Angelika came up behind them, with her mother—who was the Deputy Head. She'd been helping Ms Mountain arrange the Arts Explosion.

'Hello, Lizzie and Tyler!' Angelika's mum gave them a big smile. 'And Robo! *He's* got a really important job today!'

Tyler nodded 'He's very excited about it.'

Lizzie glanced at the stewards, but they weren't laughing. They were looking interested.

'So what's this important job?' one of them said.

Tyler grinned importantly. 'Robo's making the official Arts Explosion film. He's going round the field filming all the workshops—he's already got the route in his memory. Our friend Ethan's going to edit the film, so it can go on the school website.'

'Go straight through!' the steward said with a grin. 'We don't want the robot missing anything!'

Tyler and Robo hurried through the gate, with Lizzie and Angelika close behind.

Lizzie nudged Tyler. 'So switch on Robo's camera. Hurry, or you'll miss your workshop.'

'Don't *nag*.' Tyler pressed a switch on Robo's chest and the robot's big, shiny body turned from side to side, panning round the field.

Checking location said his mechanical voice.

'Is that all you have to do?' Angelika said.

Tyler nodded. 'He'll do the rest by himself. Watch.'

With a couple of clicks, Robo rolled off through the crowd. Lizzie could hear kids from the other schools whispering as he went past.

What's that?

Is it someone dressed up?

'Idiots,' Tyler muttered scornfully. 'Haven't they ever seen a robot before?'

'They might not—' Angelika started. Then two girls in front turned round to look at Robo and she let out a loud squeal. 'Hey! Hannah! Zainab! OVER HERE!' She began jumping up and down, waving her arms in the air.

The two girls looked past Robo—and *they* started squealing and jumping up and down too.

'Angie! It's *you*!'

'Is *this* the school where your mum works?'

They raced towards Angelika and they all met in a huge, three-way hug. When they finally let each other go, Angelika turned and gave Lizzie and Tyler a huge grin.

'Hannah and Zainab are in my dance class! And they've signed up for the dance workshop here! Isn't that fantastic? We can spend the *whole day* together!' She linked arms with her friends and the three of them walked off across the field, making for the dance workshop tent.

Tyler shook his head. 'Why are girls so *noisy*?'

'Why do boys always waste time?' Lizzie gave him a push. 'If you don't hurry up, you're going to miss the magic workshop. Go *on*, Ty!'

'See you at lunchtime.' Tyler shot off towards the big tent where the magic workshop was about to start, and Lizzie stood on her own, taking a deep breath.

There were lots of workshops she could have done. She loved making cakes and the baking workshop looked fantastic. Or she could have done gymnastics. Or graffiti. Or joined in the poetry slam. They all sounded great.

But she'd known which one she really wanted to do, from the moment she read its name: *Murder and Mystery: write your own detective thriller*. That had to be the most exciting workshop of all.

Only . . . she felt a bit nervous about it. Suppose all the other kids were brilliant writers? Suppose the man leading the workshop said her story was rubbish? Or—even worse—suppose she couldn't think of a story at all?

She walked slowly across the field. It was getting

emptier as the workshops started. She heard loud shouts of *Abracadabra* from one of the tents she passed (Tyler must be in there) and a frenzy of drumbeats from another (that had to be Blake).

By the time she reached the right place, her workshop was just about to start and a man's voice was booming from inside the tent.

'Good morning, kids! You may have heard of me. I'm Hal Nolan!'

Lizzie's mouth dropped open. *Hal Nolan?* The local bookshop window was full of his books. And they were serialized on TV. He was *famous!* That made her even more nervous and she hesitated outside the tent.

There was no danger of missing anything. Hal Nolan had a *very* loud voice.

'Clues!' he boomed. 'They're the vital thing. Choose the clues that are going to lead your detective to the right answer, and then—' he paused dramatically '—then hide the *real* clues, by adding in *fake* ones. So you're going to need lots and lots of—what?'

'Clues!' said a dozen voices.

'That's right! So give me some ideas for great clues.'

There was some muttering from the audience and then people started calling out suggestions.

'Footmarks!'

'Fingerprints!'

'Strange noises in the night!'

'Boring, boring, BORING!' Hal Nolan said scornfully. 'They've all been done a hundred times before. You need something *new*. Something that doesn't shout "Clue!"

the moment people read about it. That's what you're going to look for now. Take your notebooks and pens and go round the field, writing down as many possible clues as you can find. You've got ten minutes!'

There was a lot of chattering and shoving as people came flooding out of the tent, spreading across the field to hunt for ideas. That didn't sound too difficult. Lizzie walked round to the entrance of the tent and stuck her head inside.

Hal Nolan was sitting on the edge of the stage, eating a bar of chocolate. When he saw Lizzie, he pulled a face. 'You're too late,' he said. 'They're all out on a quest, looking for clues.'

'I heard,' Lizzie said. 'I'm going too. Sorry I missed the beginning.'

He waved an arm. 'No problem. Off you go.' And he took another bite of his chocolate bar.

Lizzie pulled out her notebook. *Chocolate bar with toothmarks* she wrote on the first page. Then she hurried out of the tent and started looking around.

All the other kids from the detective workshop were wandering around in the middle of the field, staring down at the grass or up into the sky. As far as Lizzie could see, they weren't going to spot anything except footprints and birds. She wanted something *different*.

Slipping round behind the tent, she started working her way along the edge of the field. There wasn't much space between the tents and the hedge, and she got scratched several times, but she found some interesting things to write down:

chocolate bar with toothmarks
two long black feathers
a little pile of empty snail shells
an old railway ticket
a small toy tractor, with three wheels missing

As she wrote the last few words, she took out her phone to check the time. Only one minute left. She could hardly believe she'd been looking so long, but when she peered between the tents she saw that she was almost halfway round the field.

There was no time to struggle back along the hedge. She'd have to run straight across the field. Pushing the notebook into her pocket, she started edging her way between the two nearest tents, being careful not to trip over the guy ropes.

She had only taken a couple of steps when she heard a voice coming from inside the small tent on her right. It was a very quiet voice—so quiet that she could only just make out the words—but there was something about it that stopped her where she was. The voice slipped through the wall of the tent like small snake slithering between long blades of grass.

'I will obey all your instructions.'

That was all. Just six words that didn't mean much on their own. But there was something about the voice that made Lizzie shiver. Something . . . wrong. She knew it was a person speaking, but in a strange, horrible way it was like listening to . . . to . . .

Robo.

That was it. The person in the tent was talking like a robot.

Was it someone acting? She stepped over the last guy rope and went round to the front, to see if there was a drama workshop going on in the tent.

There wasn't. The front flap of the tent was laced shut and there was a notice taped to one side:

NO ADMITTANCE

Standing very still, she listened for a few seconds, but there were no more sounds. She wanted to see who would come out of the tent, but if she waited she would miss the rest of her workshop.

And it was nothing. Of *course* it was nothing. Maybe there wasn't really a voice at all. Perhaps she'd just imagined it.

As she hesitated, half a dozen people hurried past her, waving their notebooks and chatting about the clues they'd found. She let them sweep her along, trying to forget the voice and concentrate on what she was supposed to be doing.

Hal Nolan had finished his chocolate bar and he was ready for them all. 'Found some good clues? Excellent! Now let's use them to build fantastic plots. First of all . . .'

After that, there was no time to think about anything else except the workshop. He had them drawing up plans, collecting mysterious words, working out what they needed to research, and miming how their characters would walk. Lizzie's head was spinning, but it all made wonderful sense. *So that's how he does it!* she was thinking. *Yes, I can do that too.*

By the end of the session, she had the outline of a wonderful, gruesome mystery.

So had all the others. They charged out of the tent, chattering about their characters and clues and which bits they were going to write first. Sounding loud and excited and very, very happy.

It is *like an explosion,* Lizzie thought. *Just the way Ms Mountain wanted it to be.*

She was just as excited as everyone else, but she had one more thing to write down before she left the tent. She had no idea how to fit it into her story, but she didn't want to forget it. Opening her notebook again, she added it to her list of clues:

chocolate bar with toothmarks
two long black feathers
a little pile of empty snail shells
an old railway ticket
a small toy tractor, with three wheels missing
and
a voice saying, 'I will obey all your instructions.'

4

MEGA CONFERENCE

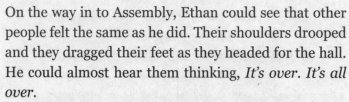

When the CGI workshop finished, Ethan and Jatinder were desperate to keep going. They'd built some amazing avatars and drafted plans for a brilliant new world. They spent the rest of the weekend messaging backwards and forwards as they worked on it, and on Sunday evening Auntie Beryl had to shout at Ethan three times to get him to go to bed.

But then it was Monday. And the Arts Explosion was over. As Ethan cycled to school on Monday morning, the whole world felt grey. The rest of the term was going to be really, really DULL.

He still had a lot to learn about Ms Mountain.

On the way in to Assembly, Ethan could see that other people felt the same as he did. Their shoulders drooped and they dragged their feet as they headed for the hall. He could almost hear them thinking, *It's over. It's all over.*

Ms Mountain was already up on the stage. She beckoned impatiently, hurrying them along as if there was no time to waste. The last people hadn't even sat down when she started talking.

'So,' she said, 'was the Arts Explosion good?' She grinned as a roar went up, from all over the hall. 'Did you like the AE Orchestra!'

'YAY!' yelled Blake, waving his arms in the air.

'And the Amazing Magic Show!'

There was a huge cheer from a dozen different places in the hall. Ethan could hear Tyler shouting louder than anyone else.

Ms Mountain beamed down at them all. 'And *fifteen* CGI partnerships!'

'YESSS!' Suddenly Ethan found himself cheering too.

'And the Volcano Dancers . . . and the Graffiti Explosion . . .'

The list went on and on, with huge cheers for each one. By the time it finished, there was an excited buzz all over the hall.

'Well, those things are just the start,' Ms Mountain said. 'On Friday, I'm running a Mega Conference with the Heads of all the other schools, to kick-start a galaxy of glittering new projects. The only downside is—' She stopped and looked round.

Everyone stared up at her, wondering what she was going to say.

She paused for a moment, looking very solemn. Then she grinned. 'The Mega Conference is going to be here. So there won't be any school on Friday. You've all got the day off.'

That raised the biggest cheer of all.

But not everyone was happy. Auntie Beryl was annoyed when Ethan brought home the letter about the Mega Conference.

'You mean there's no school on Friday?' She put on her glasses and read it, frowning down at the paper. 'What am I supposed to do about that? I have to be at work.'

'We can go to St Asaph's if we haven't got anywhere else.' Ethan pointed at the bottom of the letter. 'But Lizzie says I can go to their house instead, if it's OK with you.'

'Well . . . it's very kind of Lizzie's parents,' Auntie Beryl said carefully. 'But don't they have to go to work too?'

'Her dad does. But not her mum. She's at home all the time, because she hasn't been well. Lizzie says she'd love to see us, and I could help look after Tyler. Angelika and Blake are coming too. And there's the park—'

Auntie Beryl thought about it. 'Well . . . if you're sure. But it's not fair to expect Lizzie's mother to feed you all. I'll cook something for you to take.'

'I'll be on my bike,' Ethan said cautiously. 'I might not be able to carry much.'

Auntie Beryl brushed that away. 'I'll pack it up for you. Would you like a lasagne for lunch?'

That sounded much too easy to spill. But Ethan knew he had to take something. Auntie Beryl hated the idea of *imposing on people*.

'How about some of your brownies?' he said. 'They all love those. Angelika says they're the best brownies in the entire world.'

Auntie Beryl beamed. 'I'll bake a double batch. That should be enough to go round.'

Perfect! Ethan thought, as she bustled off to the kitchen. Brownies would be easy to carry. And it didn't matter how many she cooked. Blake would finish off what the rest of them couldn't manage. He grinned and went into his bedroom, to message Jatinder about their game.

As he turned on his computer, he remembered Robo's video from the Arts Explosion. He was supposed to be editing it, for the school website. He hesitated for a moment, looking at the folder. He ought to do it, but it was going to be a long, boring job. It could wait a few more days.

He opened up his game folder instead.

On Friday, he was still eating his breakfast when Auntie Beryl pulled on her coat and picked up her car keys.

'Your brownies are over there.' She waved at two large plastic boxes on the worktop. 'There should be enough for everyone. Don't forget to lock the front door when you go.'

Ethan nodded, with his mouth full of cereal. When Auntie Beryl had gone, he decided he had time for some toast, so he pulled the toaster out of the cupboard, pushing the stack of boxes away to make room for it. While the bread was toasting, he looked at the jars of spread. Peanut butter? Or jam?

In the end, he had both. *And* another piece of toast. He sat and munched, thinking about his game, until he looked up at the clock and saw it was almost half past nine.

Help! If he didn't get going soon, Lizzie's mum might call Auntie Beryl, to make sure he was coming. That would put Auntie Beryl in a flap. He jumped up, dropped his plate into the dishwasher, and pulled on his trainers.

There was something he had to remember. What had Auntie Beryl said? He glanced round the kitchen and saw his keys on the worktop. That must be it. *Don't forget to lock the front door when you go.* He grabbed the keys, put on his coat, and headed out of the flat.

By twenty-five to ten, he was on his bike, cycling away down the road.

The quickest route to Lizzie's went straight past the school. He cycled that way, forgetting about the Mega Conference, and as he came round the corner by the school, he hit a traffic jam. Cars were queuing all down the road, waiting to turn right into the school car park.

Getting off his bike, Ethan started pushing it along the pavement. As he drew level with the school gate, the traffic jam began to clear and a line of cars drove past him, into the car park. One, two, three . . .

The fourth one was the black Rolls that had almost knocked him down on Saturday. It slid smoothly by, so close that he could have touched the round, golden symbol on its gleaming black side. The driver was the same red-haired man as before and there was a tall figure sitting in the back, barely visible through the smoked glass.

Ethan watched as it pulled into the best parking space. Should he go across and complain about what had happened on Saturday? As he hesitated, the driver got out and walked round to the other side of the car, to open the back door.

Before he could see who got out, another car stopped in front of him. It hooted cheerfully and the driver's window went down.

'Ethan!' said a loud, cheerful voice. It was Mr Ramsey, the Head of his old school. 'How are you doing?'

Ethan grinned. He liked Mr Ramsey. 'Everything's great, thank you. Jatinder and I did the computer graphics workshop at the Arts Explosion. It was brilliant!'

Mr Ramsey grinned back. 'You two are a great team. Glad you're staying in touch.'

He obviously wanted to chat, but a car hooted behind him and he gave an apologetic wave and drove off into the school car park. Ethan looked back at the black Rolls, but the driver and the passenger had both disappeared.

'A black Rolls?' Blake said. 'That sounds really cool!'

They were all sitting in the park next to Lizzie and Tyler's house, drinking some of Angelika's homemade lemonade. It was delicious.

'Maybe the Rolls was bringing one of the speakers,' Lizzie said.

Angelika nodded. 'I bet Ms Mountain's invited *loads* of speakers.'

'Sounds boring,' Blake said. He stuck out his tongue and licked the inside of his empty glass. 'This is brilliant lemonade, Angie. Ever thought of opening your own drinks stall?'

'Ha ha, very funny,' Angelika said sourly. She thumped his arm—and then squealed and rubbed her hand. Hitting Blake was like punching Stonehenge.

Tyler shook his head at Blake. 'Don't tease her. You know how she *hated* running that coffee stall last term.'

'She made fantastic hot chocolate though.' Blake held out his glass for more lemonade.

'Except the one she made for the Prime Minister.' Tyler grinned. 'Remember?'

'Of course I remember,' Blake said. 'D'you think I'm stupid?'

Tyler opened his eyes very wide. 'We-e-ell . . .'

Blake growled and Tyler jumped up and shot across the park, laughing so much he could hardly run straight.

'Everything's so different from last term,' Lizzie said. 'What do you think Ms Mountain will do next?'

Ethan shook his head. 'Could be *anything*. How about a Science Explosion? That would be great.'

'A *Food* Explosion!' Blake said, licking his lips.

'Yes!' Angelika clapped her hands. 'We could have a Mega Baking Day. Or Cooking Round the World—with stalls for all the different countries. Or—'

'Stop it!' Tyler shouted, from the other side of the bandstand. 'You're making me hungry. And lunch isn't for ages.'

Ethan sat up suddenly. Remembering. 'Auntie Beryl gave me a snack to bring—and I've left it at home!'

'Never mind,' Lizzie said. 'We'll be fine until lunchtime.'

Ethan shook his head. 'You don't understand. Auntie Beryl's going to be really upset if we don't eat her brownies. I'll have to go back and get them. What's the time?'

Angelika looked at her phone. 'Just gone quarter past ten.'

'If I go now, I'll be back by eleven.' Ethan scrambled up. 'Then we can have a snack.'

Blake beamed. 'I love your Auntie Beryl's brownies!'

All the others laughed, but Ethan didn't even hear. He was already wheeling his bike towards the park gates.

He went back the same way he'd come. Now the conference had started, he wasn't expecting much traffic. As he came round the corner into Hazelbrook Road, he looked sideways, to see if he could spot the mysterious Rolls-Royce again.

It wasn't there.

There were no cars there at all. The school car park was completely empty.

He was so surprised that he stopped and got off his bike. Less than an hour ago there had been dozens of cars, queuing to get in. Now there were none. And there were no lights on in the school building.

How could the Conference be over already? What kind of Mega Conference starts at ten o'clock and finishes before eleven?

Ethan stared across at the car park, trying to think of a sensible explanation, but he couldn't. Why were they missing a whole day of school—for something that was over already?

'Maybe there was only one speaker,' Lizzie said, when he got back to the park.

Angelika shook her head. 'Conferences aren't *like* that.' She waved the brownie she was holding. 'My mum's been to loads of conferences and they went on all day. More than one day sometimes. And she says it's not just about the speakers. The best bit is chatting to other people and swapping ideas, in the coffee break.'

'They can't have had a coffee break today,' Lizzie said. 'Unless that was *all* they did.'

Ethan frowned. 'So why did we have to miss a whole day of school?'

'Maybe they just didn't want us around.' Tyler was getting bored. He jumped up and tugged at Blake's shoulder. 'Let's play football. Bet you can't tackle me!'

He grabbed the ball Blake had brought, kicked it across the park ,and ran after it. Blake raced after him, and Lizzie grinned.

'That's brilliant. Tyler used to be really scared of Blake, because he was such a bully.'

'*Blake?*' Angelika hadn't been at Hazelbrook long

enough to remember that. 'But he's a pussycat. Isn't he, Ethan?'

'Hmm?' Ethan wasn't listening. He was still puzzling over why the Mega Conference had been so short. Words kept running through his head.

. . . My mum's been to loads of conferences and they went on all day . . .

. . . They can't have had a coffee break today . . .

. . . Maybe they just didn't want us around . . .

Something wasn't right. But he just couldn't work out what it was . . .

5

THE NEXT BIG THING

Lizzie was thinking the same thing. It was all very strange. How come the Heads had all vanished so quickly? Had they gone off to visit each other's schools? Or made a plan and gone off to work out the details? Or—

She couldn't really think of a sensible explanation. But, with Ms Mountain, nothing was the way they expected. Why should the Mega Conference be any different? And who cared what the Heads were up to, anyway? There was a much more important question.

What was Ms Mountain going to do next?

That was what everyone kept asking on Monday morning. *What's Ms Mountain's new plan?* And they didn't have to wait long for an answer. When they walked into Assembly, there was a video running on the big screen above the stage.

Lizzie stared at it as she sat down. It must have been filmed from a helicopter or a drone, high above the ground. It showed a wild, rocky island, with a jagged black mountain rearing up in the middle. Below the mountain, the sea crashed against tall cliffs, throwing up huge waves of spray and sending clouds of sea birds whirling into the air.

Angelika looked up at the screen and shivered. 'How *horrible!*'

'Horrible?' Lizzie shook her head. 'It's brilliant! Imagine being right at the top of that mountain! Or up on the cliffs, with the spray hitting your face. It would make you feel really *alive.*'

'It would make *me* feel petrified.' Angelika's voice was shaking. 'I hate heights. And I always get seasick in boats.' She looked away from the screen and started talking to Ethan.

Lizzie couldn't take her eyes off the pictures. What would it be like to stand on that mountain, feeling the wind on your face? To hear the thunder of the sea against the cliffs? Would there be caves to explore? And rocks where seals came to bask in the sunshine? Maybe there would be dolphins swimming past, and puffins popping their heads out of burrows.

She'd always dreamed of visiting an island like that. One that was so small you could walk round it in a couple of hours, but where you would never get tired of watching the wildlife and the changing sea and sky. If only . . .

Ms Mountain bounced on to the stage, waving her arms and beaming down at them all. 'Isn't it a fantastic island?' she said. 'Would you like to be there? Swimming with dolphins? Climbing the cliffs? Kayaking in the sea and camping out under the stars?'

'YEEESSSS!' The shout came from all over the hall.

Ms Mountain laughed and held up her hands. 'Well, five lucky people will do just that. There's going to be a competition . . .' She paused and looked around.

Lizzie could hardly breathe. What was she going to say?

'You all did brilliant work at the Arts Explosion.' Ms Mountain beamed down at them. 'Now there's going to be a competition—for presentations based on those workshops. And the five people who send me the best presentations—five *lucky* people—will win a *free* trip to this uninhabited Scottish island.' She waved her hand at the screen behind her. 'Those five people will be doing all the things I've talked about—climbing and abseiling and kayaking and camping—with an expert leader to help them.'

Lizzie could feel her heart thumping. The island—the beautiful, exciting island—had her under its spell and she couldn't take her eyes off the pictures on the screen. She had to be one of those lucky five people. She *had* to be.

'The work you did at the Arts Explosion is just your starting point,' Ms Mountain said. 'You can use *whatever resources you like* to make your work a winner. Think outside the box! Give me something sensational! And when you've finished, send me a video. But you haven't got long. It must arrive by midnight this coming Sunday. Got it?'

'YES!' The shout went up from all over the hall.

'Then off you go. Good luck, everyone.'

They were supposed to file out in silence, but there was no chance of that. Everyone was much too excited about the island. People were thinking out loud and whispering their plans to each other.

Blake was sure he was going to be one of the five lucky people. 'Just wait till Ms Mountain hears my drumming solo!' he said. 'It's going to be better than anyone else's presentation! And Ms Mountain's going to need someone like me on the island.' He flexed his muscles. 'Someone *strong* who can carry supplies and chop down trees.'

Tyler came up beside them and tugged at Lizzie's sleeve. 'I *have* to go to the island,' he said. 'It looks like the best thing ever.'

'Better think of some great magic, then,' Lizzie said.

'I already have!' Tyler grinned. 'And I'm going to get Robo to help me. Then I can tell Ms Mountain he has to come to the island too, because he's part of the presentation.' He bounced off down the corridor.

He looked as though he had a really good idea. And Blake's solo would probably be fantastic too. Lizzie started feeling anxious. How could she compete with things like magic and drumming? All she had was the detective story she'd started at the Arts Explosion. How could she make that really special?

She couldn't concentrate on any of her lessons that morning. All she wanted to do was go somewhere on her own, so she could start writing. As soon as the bell sounded for break, she headed off to the library.

But lots of other people had had the same idea and all the seats were full.

Most people were bent over piles of books, scribbling notes. But a couple of girls were fooling about, leaning over a newspaper and giggling. When Mr Bains saw

Lizzie hesitating in the doorway, he went across and chivvied the girls away.

'If you don't want to work, leave the places for people who do,' he said. 'Go outside and get some fresh air.'

The girls went off, in a mixture of giggles and grumbling. Lizzie gave Mr Bains a grateful smile and went to sit in one of the empty chairs. As she sat down, she glanced at the newspaper to see what had made those girls laugh. She saw the headline straight away.

OUR SCHOOL'S A CIRCUS!

Underneath the headline was a picture of two men on stilts and a large, middle-aged woman dressed as a clown. All three of them looked very unhappy. What was that all about? Lizzie read the rest of the article.

Staff at Addington Street School have been asked to dress as circus performers. 'This will reduce tension in the school,' explained Bill Jackson (54) the Head Teacher. 'Our pupils are getting ready for important exams and they are in danger of taking themselves too seriously.

'Instead of revision, I have asked the staff to hold classes in circus skills and prepare the pupils for a grand circus performance the day after the end of the exams. Keep clowning, kids! Don't worry about your exams!'

Lizzie shook her head. It had to be some kind of joke. She pushed the paper away and took a notebook out of her bag. She hadn't got any time to waste reading newspapers. She needed to work on her detective story.

6

A WEIRD CONVERSATION

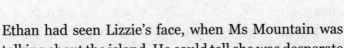

Ethan had seen Lizzie's face, when Ms Mountain was talking about the island. He could tell she was desperate to be one of the five people who went on the trip.

He wasn't so sure about it. Yes, the island looked beautiful—on the screen. But what would it be like in real life? If the wind was as fierce as it seemed, it would be very hard to pitch any tents. He didn't fancy climbing the mountain in a gale either. And swimming with dolphins sounded amazing—but wouldn't the sea be freezing cold?

He was planning to talk to Lizzie at break, but she shot out of the classroom the moment break started. He was going to go after her, but he met Angelika's mother outside the classroom door.

'Ethan,' she said. 'I was just coming to find you.'

'Hi.' Ethan grinned at her.

She grinned back, but she obviously didn't have time to chat. She was obviously on a Deputy Head-type mission. 'Ms Martin wants to see you in her office,' she said. 'Straight away.'

'Me?' Ethan was surprised. What could Ms Mountain have to say to *him*?

'Off you go. Don't keep her waiting.'

Ethan set off down the corridor, trying to guess what it was all about. He couldn't think of anything he'd done wrong.

When he knocked on the door of Ms Mountain's office, she called, 'Come in!' in a loud, cheerful voice. That didn't *sound* like trouble. Ethan pushed the door open.

'Ethan! Fantastic!' Ms Mountain waved at the chair on the other side of her desk. 'Take a seat. I'm hoping you can help me solve a problem.'

'*Me*?' Ethan blinked at her as he sat down.

'I think you're the one to do it.' Ms Mountain gave him a beaming smile. 'But I need to ask you something first. How do you feel about the island? Are you desperate to be one of the five lucky people who go on the trip?'

That was a peculiar question. What did she want him to say?

'I—er—it's an interesting plan,' Ethan muttered.

Ms Mountain leaned across the desk, staring into his eyes. 'Be honest. How do you *really* feel about it?'

'The island looks a bit . . . rugged,' Ethan said carefully. 'And very windy. I've never been camping, but it seems like a difficult place to pitch a tent.'

'Ah,' Ms Mountain said. She leaned back in her chair. 'You mean you're not keen on the idea?'

Ethan looked down at his hands. 'Not as keen as some people.'

Ms Mountain gave him an odd little smile. 'Not as keen as . . . Lizzie Warren, for example?'

Ethan didn't know what to say.

Ms Mountain gave a little nod. 'Lizzie Warren is a good, hard-working girl. I know her mother isn't well, and Lizzie takes a lot of responsibility for her brother. She deserves something nice—like going on the island trip. But I can't put her in the top five just because I want her to go. That wouldn't be fair. She has to produce a brilliant presentation. Something that makes her a clear winner. And that's where you can help.'

'*Me?*' Ethan stared.

Ms Mountain nodded. 'You're the perfect person. Lizzie will be writing a detective story—because that was the workshop she did at the Arts Explosion. She's a very good writer, but whatever she produces will just be words on a page. Unless you help her.'

'What can *I* do?' Ethan said.

'Computer graphics!' Ms Mountain gave him a big grin. 'I've seen the project you did in your workshop. It's stunning. If you can link something like that to the story Lizzie writes, you could make it spectacular.'

'But—wouldn't that be cheating?'

'Weren't you listening in Assembly?' Ms Mountain grinned again. 'I told you all to *think outside the box* and use all the resources you can find. Some people will be getting help from their families. Or their libraries. Or the internet. *You* can be a resource for Lizzie. Bringing her story to life.'

Ethan thought about it. Yes, he could do that. Whatever Lizzie's story was like, he could produce some graphics to go with it. But . . . He looked up at

Ms Mountain. 'Suppose she doesn't want any help?'

'Then you'll need to persuade her,' Ms Mountain said. 'That shouldn't be hard—if she *really* wants to go.'

Oh, she wants to go all right, Ethan thought. He remembered her face staring up at the screen. If she wasn't chosen, she would be devastated.

But she *would* be chosen. He was going to make sure of that! He looked up at Ms Mountain. 'I'll do it!' he said.

Ms Mountain gave him a long, careful look. 'You do realize,' she said, 'that it means giving up your own chance of going? I can't pick *two* presentations with stunning computer graphics. That might cause trouble with other people's parents.'

Like Blake's, Ethan thought. They were bound to complain if Blake didn't get chosen. He shrugged. 'That's OK. I don't mind.'

'Excellent!' Ms Mountain gave a small, satisfied nod. 'And . . . maybe it's best if you don't tell Lizzie you've spoken to me. Keep that a secret. Let her think it's your own idea to help her.'

Ethan nodded—though he couldn't see why it mattered. 'OK. I won't say anything.'

Ms Mountain beamed at him. 'Off you go, then. You've got a lot to do!'

Ethan went out with his brain buzzing. He couldn't wait to read Lizzie's story. But how could he offer to help without making her wonder why . . .?

He needn't have worried about that. At lunchtime, Angelika gave him the perfect opportunity.

She and Lizzie were sitting with him when Blake came swaggering into the canteen. He persuaded the dinner ladies to give him twice as much food as everyone else and then charged across to sit at their table.

'My drum concert is going to be brilliant!' he announced, digging a fork into one of his six sausages. 'I've been planning it all the morning. And I've got a great name for it. *Island Thunder*.'

Angelika raised her eyebrows. 'That sounds exhausting—for the audience. I hope you're having refreshments afterwards.'

'What?' Blake put his fork down. '*Refreshments?*'

'Of course.' Angelika nodded. 'It won't be a proper concert without refreshments in the interval.'

Was she teasing Blake? Ethan wasn't sure. She didn't *sound* as if she was joking.

Blake frowned. 'How can I do refreshments if I'm playing the drums? I'd have to have someone to help me. Someone—' His frown cleared suddenly. 'Someone like *you*, Angie. You can do the refreshments for me!'

'*Me?*' Angelika tossed her hair. 'What makes you think I'm going to help *you*, Blake Vinney?'

'You'll love it.' Blake picked the fork up. 'I'll give you a free ticket to the concert.'

Angelika shuddered. 'I don't know why you want to go to the island anyway. I felt seasick just looking at the pictures.'

'Then you might as well help me.' Blake said

cheerfully. He started chewing again.

Angelika hesitated, as if she was making up her mind—and Ethan saw his chance. He looked at Lizzie across the table. 'If Angelika helps Blake,' he said, 'I'll help *you*. How about that? I don't want to go to the island either. But I could do some graphics for your presentation. Would you like that?'

Lizzie's mouth fell open. 'That would be fantastic. Would you really?'

'Of course I will.' Ethan grinned at her. 'Anything, as long as I don't have to go to the island.'

Lizzie laughed. 'I'll email the first draft as soon as I get home.'

'Perfect. Then I can start working out what to do. And—hey!' Ethan suddenly had an idea. 'How about if I get my friend Jatinder to help? From my old school. He's a genius at CGI.'

Lizzie hesitated. 'That's lot of help. Is it fair?'

'You heard what Ms Mountain said. *Use whatever resources you like! Think outside the box!*' Ethan grinned again. 'Send the story over and I'll go and talk to Jatinder this evening.'

7

LIZZIE'S STORY

Lizzie was very excited. If Ethan was going to help her—if Ethan *and his friend Jatinder* were going to help her—she would have a chance of producing something extra-special. Special enough to win her a trip to the island.

The afternoon seemed very long. She couldn't concentrate on Maths or History. All she could think of was getting home and starting work on her story. At the end of the day, she didn't hang around at the gates, waiting for Tyler to come and join her. She went to find him in his classroom and hassled him to get ready faster.

Tyler didn't mind. He was just as keen to get home as she was. 'I've got a fantastic plan for my magic show!' he said as they walked off down the road. 'I'm going to *saw Robo in half*. Isn't that genius?'

'We-ell.' Lizzie raised her eyebrows. 'Are you sure you can put him back together again?'

'Of course I can! It's just a trick, Liz. You don't actually . . .'

Tyler launched into a long explanation, but Lizzie didn't really listen. She was busy trying to remember the story she'd started at the Arts Explosion. Could she just carry on and finish it, or would she have to start all over again—and write something much better?

It didn't take long to decide. The moment she got home from school, she found the three crumpled pages she'd written in the workshop and sat on her bed reading them. It wasn't much. Two of the pages were covered with the first part of her story, and the third one had the list of clues:

chocolate bar with toothmarks
two long black feathers
a little pile of empty snail shells
an old railway ticket
a small toy tractor, with three wheels missing
a voice saying, 'I will obey all your instructions.'

She hadn't managed to fit all the clues into her story so far. The feathers and the railway ticket were easy, and she thought she could do something with the chocolate and the snail shells. Maybe even the toy tractor.

But what about the voice? What could she do with that?

She remembered the sound of it, very clearly. No normal person would talk like that. Could she give the words to a ghost? A zombie? Whatever she did, the voice was so weird it would make what she'd written so far seem dull and ordinary.

And it wasn't a ghost or a zombie, because it was

a real voice. She'd *heard* it. And one of the things that made it creepy was that it was a bit familiar. Familiar—and *wrong*. That was why she couldn't get it out of her mind. She needed to know whose voice it was. But there didn't seem to be any way of finding out.

She was puzzling over that, when Tyler came blundering into the room, with Robo rolling along behind him.

'I'm stuck,' he wailed. 'I can't think how to make a box for sawing Robo in half.'

Lizzie shook her head. She didn't want to waste time thinking about magic. 'So don't do that. Your show will be fine without Robo.'

'No it won't!' Tyler wailed. 'He *has* to be in the show. Or he won't be able to come to the island with me.'

'Ty, you can't take Robo *everywhere*.'

'He's *got* to come!' Tyler said fiercely. 'He'll be really upset if I go to the island without him.'

'Oh Ty—' *Robo hasn't GOT any feelings. He's a ROBOT!* That was what Lizzie wanted to say. But there was no point. Tyler wouldn't listen. 'There must be another way to fit him into your show,' she said. 'What did you do with him in your Arts Explosion workshop?'

'He didn't come to the workshop. Don't you remember? He was doing the video.'

'The—?' For a second Lizzie couldn't think what Tyler was talking about. Then she remembered—and it almost took her breath away.

Robo had spent the whole day rolling round the field *videoing what was going on*. And that meant that maybe—just maybe—he might have filmed someone going into that little tent. Or someone coming out.

The person with the mysterious voice.

'Oh, the *video*,' she said, trying not to sound too interested, because she didn't want to explain about the voice. 'We never watched it, did we? Has Robo still got it?'

'I think so.' Tyler shrugged. 'Ethan copied it on to his computer, to edit it, but I don't think he deleted Robo's copy. Why?'

'Nothing important,' Lizzie said airily. 'I just wondered . . . something about the clues for my story. Could I watch it now?'

'It's really boring.' Tyler pulled a face. 'Just film of people walking in and out of tents.'

Lizzie's heart thudded. 'You don't have to watch,' she said, trying to sound casual. 'But I'd like to have a quick look. Why don't you leave Robo here and—' she thought quickly '—and go and talk to Dad about that box you need. He might make one for you.'

'Do you think he would?' Tyler's eyes gleamed. 'That would be amazing!' He rushed out of the room, calling, 'Dad! Dad! I need some help.'

Lizzie knelt down in front of Robo and looked at his control panel. She didn't know much about how he worked, but she could find the menu. She tapped the control panel and Robo lifted his big, square head.

Good afternoon, he said. **The time is seventeen fifty-three. I await your instructions.**

Lizzie tapped again. It was easy to set up the video

and she sat down on her bed to watch. For the first couple of minutes, it was just a jumble of tents and people. Then it settled down to a pattern as Robo started rolling across the field, turning left and right as he went.

Lizzie saw the tent labelled **MAGIC WORKSHOP**, with Tyler queuing outside. Then another tent full of musical instruments—with Blake on one side, bashing away at a drum kit. And a few seconds later, three girls walked across the field.

Lizzie thought it was Angelika, with the two girls from her old school. But before she could be sure, the video changed as Robo spun round. Now she was looking at the field entrance, with the school car park beyond it. A big, black car with a golden symbol on its side was pulling into the car park.

Who cared about cars? Lizzie fast-forwarded impatiently. Now there were kids queuing to get into their workshops. They kept waving at Robo and crowding round to take selfies. But that didn't last long. Soon, the workshops started, and there was nothing to see except a big, empty space with tents all round the edge.

She fast-forwarded again, staring hard at the screen, and suddenly she saw—herself. She was coming from behind the tents, walking between two of them. That was it! That was the *exact moment* she wanted. Quickly, she paused the video.

Robo must have been filming from the other side of the field, because the tents looked very small. The figure walking between them was even smaller, but it was her. She knew it was. That was where she had been a second before she heard the creepy voice.

The owner of the voice must have been inside the little tent on the left. So if she started the video again, she just . . . might . . . see . . . Holding her breath, she set it going and watched herself walking forward and then turning right, heading back to her writing workshop.

A moment later, someone lifted the flap of the little tent on the left. For a split second, there was a flash of red. A figure coming out of the tent. But it was only a glimpse. The next moment, Robo turned away and the camera panned round the field. But Lizzie didn't care.

She'd found the picture she was looking for.

Going back to the place where the tent started opening, she moved the video forward, frame by frame. When she reached the frame where the figure appeared, she zoomed in on it. But that just made everything blurred. All she could see was a featureless blob in red clothes.

There must be a way to make the picture clearer. She could ask Ethan, but—how could she explain why it mattered? *I heard a really creepy voice?* That just sounded silly. He wouldn't understand unless he knew what it *felt* like to hear the voice. If she could only get that across . . .

Suddenly she got it. The perfect way!

Grabbing her paper, Lizzie crossed out everything she'd written before. Then she wrote a brand-new title across the top of a clean sheet of paper:

The Mysterious Voice.

8

YOU'RE NO GOOD!

Ethan couldn't wait to read Lizzie's story. He wanted to start work on the graphics, but first he needed to know what the story was about.

It was very unsettling. He couldn't start anything else, because he would have to stop when Lizzie emailed her story—and that could happen at any moment. And he couldn't get hold of Jatinder, to ask him to help. Jatinder seemed to have turned his phone off.

Which he *never* did.

After he'd hung around for half an hour, Ethan couldn't stand it any longer. He went into the kitchen to find Auntie Beryl.

'I'm going round to Jatinder's house,' he said.

Auntie Beryl frowned. 'Not before tea. It's ready to go on the table.'

She wouldn't let him go out until he'd eaten every mouthful. *And* loaded the dishwasher.

'And mind you're back before dark,' she said.

As Ethan cycled off, he wondered whether Jatinder and his family had gone away. If Jatinder was on an aeroplane, that would explain why he hadn't answered those messages. But the house wasn't dark when he got there. There was a light at every window. And when he rang the doorbell, it was Jatinder who opened the door.

He looked terrible. His eyes were bloodshot and there were bags under his eyes. Ethan was shocked.

'Oh, it's you,' Jatinder said dully. 'Hi.'

'Hi,' Ethan said. 'Are you . . . OK?'

Jatinder shrugged. 'I suppose.'

'Didn't you get my messages?'

'Dad won't let me read any messages. Not till I've finished my homework. Actually—' Jatinder's eyes brightened, 'maybe you can help me.'

Jatinder asking for help? That was a first. 'What kind of homework is it?' Ethan said.

Jatinder mumbled something that sounded like *IT*.

'*What*?' Ethan couldn't believe what he was hearing. Jatinder was a *superstar* at IT. Better than the teacher. How could he possibly need any help?

'Wait till you see the homework,' Jatinder said bitterly. He stepped back to let Ethan inside and then called over his shoulder. 'Ethan's here, Dad. He's going to help me with my IT.'

They went upstairs to Jatinder's bedroom and he took a worksheet off his desk and held it out. 'Here you are. Can *you* do it?'

Ethan read the first paragraph, blinked, and read it again.

Develop a programming language suitable for AI that allows you to create new syntax and simulations, using object-oriented programming and infinite data structures.

He shook his head. 'Mr Copeland wants you

to develop a programming language for artificial intelligence? A *new* programming language? Doesn't that take years? And what does the rest of the sentence mean?'

Jatinder shrugged. 'No idea. I've had it for three days already. I tried talking to Mr Copeland yesterday, but he just told me to look on the web. He said, *If you can't do a simple thing like that, you're not as good as you think you are.*'

'But you *are* good.' Ethan was baffled. 'You're way ahead of everyone else.'

Jatinder shook his head. 'That's what I thought. But I guess I've been fooling myself. I've spent *hours* looking up all sorts of stuff, but I still don't know what to do.'

Ethan looked at the worksheet. 'What's the point of giving you impossible homework?'

'Mr Copeland says it's about *raising standards.*' Jatinder frowned. 'Mr Ramsey keeps nagging us about that. All the time.'

'*Mr Ramsey?*' Ethan couldn't believe it. 'He doesn't nag.'

'He does now,' Jatinder said. '*Everyone's* getting impossible homework. You know how Morgan loves history? Well, yesterday she was crying because Mrs Lucas had given her a medieval document. In Old French. Morgan has to answer questions about it, using other documents of the same period, and she doesn't even know what it means. And Alex—'

Before Jatinder could finish, his mother shouted

up the stairs. Ethan couldn't understand what she was saying, but Jatinder gave a gasp and ran out of the room. A second later, Ethan heard his voice from the kitchen.

'Sam's done what? *Sam?*'

For a couple of minutes, he and his mother were talking very fast. Then Jatinder came racing back upstairs. He looked stunned.

'Sam's disappeared,' he said. 'His mum just rang my mum and she's really upset. She thinks Sam's run away.'

Ethan stared. '*Sam?* Why would he do that?'

'He's left a note. About how his life is ruined and he's never coming back.'

'*Why?*' Ethan couldn't believe it.

'It's his band,' Jatinder said miserably. 'He was really excited, because they'd got an actual gig, next month. They were going to get paid and everything. So he asked Mr Wilson if they could rehearse in the music studio.'

'And Mr Wilson wouldn't let them?' Ethan guessed.

'Oh, he let them,' Jatinder said bitterly. 'He even said he'd help. But when he heard their first song he told them it was rubbish. He said Sam couldn't sing at all and he'd make a fool of himself if they went ahead with the gig.'

Ethan stared. 'But Sam's a brilliant singer.'

Jatinder nodded. 'And it's a great band. But Mr Wilson's an expert, isn't he? He used to play in a proper, professional band before he started teaching. Sam was devastated. I couldn't cheer him up—and now he's run away.'

'Can't we go and look for him?' Ethan said.

'That's why his mum rang. She's going out to hunt for him and she wants all the help she can get. I'm going to go straight round there.'

'I'll come too. Hang on while I tell Auntie Beryl.' Ethan sent her a message—just saying he was going round to Sam's—then he and Jatinder cycled off, as fast as they could.

Sam's mother was outside the house, talking on the phone. When she saw Ethan and Jatinder, she put the phone away and ran to meet them.

'Thank goodness you're here! Can you think where Sam might have gone? The police say it's too soon to worry, but it's not *like* him to run off.'

'Did he take his bike?' Ethan said.

Sam's mother shook her head. 'No, it's still here. He hasn't taken his phone either. And he hasn't got any money, because he's just bought a new guitar.'

'So he can't be far,' Jatinder said. 'Don't worry, we'll find him. OK, Ethan? Let's go different ways, so we cover more ground.'

Ethan nodded. 'And shall I ask some more people? Who can look on the other side of town?'

'That would be great,' Sam's mother said. 'But do they *know* Sam?'

'I'll send them a picture.' Ethan flicked through his photos. He found the one he'd taken with Sam and

Jatinder, on his last day at the old school, and sent it to Lizzie and Blake and Angelika.

URGENT!! Sam is missing (one on the right) Plz check park & canal.

Jatinder read the message over Ethan's shoulder. 'Good idea,' he said. 'I'll go up by the ring road.'

Ethan nodded. 'I'll check the High Street. And then call you.'

'Call me too,' Sam's mother said. 'I've got Sam's phone in my pocket.'

Jatinder frowned. 'If he hasn't taken his phone, he must be feeling really bad. Let's get out there and find him!'

'I'm on my way!' Ethan said. And they pedalled off in opposite directions.

9

ON THE TOWPATH

Lizzie had just finished her story when she heard the message arrive. She was typing an email to Ethan.

Here's my story. Is it OK? Can we talk tomorrow?

She attached the story and sent off the email. Then she picked up her phone. Before she had a chance to read Ethan's message, two more came zapping in, from Blake and Angelika.

Where shall we look first? That was Blake.

Angelika seemed to be replying to that. You do your side of the park. I'll do mine. Canal for you, Lizzie?

She flipped up to Ethan's message.

URGENT!! Sam is missing (one on the right) Plz check park & canal.

She had a quick look at the picture and then headed for the door, answering the message as she went. On my way to canal. Grabbing her coat, she called, 'Just going out for a bit. Back soon.'

No point in worrying her mum by telling her someone was missing. And best not to tell Tyler either. He would only slow her down. If she went on her own, it would only take half an hour to check the canal and she could do the whole thing before it started getting dark.

She headed down Liddell Street, towards the canal bridge. As she reached it, she heard a peculiar noise below her, on the towpath.

Clang, clang, clang.

Leaning over the parapet, she looked down and saw a boy walking slowly towards the bridge, with his head down and his hands in his pockets. And every time he took a step, he kicked out at the railings beside the towpath. *Clang, clang, clang.*

Whipping out her phone, Lizzie checked the photo Ethan had sent. Then she looked down again. It was Sam all right. And he looked wretched. His shoulders drooped, his head was hanging down, and every kick he aimed at the railings was harder than the last one. *Clang, clang, CLANG.*

Lizzie sent a quick message. Found him. Canal towpath under Liddell Bridge. Then she looked down again. Sam had walked under the bridge. Now he was trudging on down the towpath, towards the next one.

She had to follow him. As quietly as she could. If he heard her, he might run off—and all the bridges had steps leading up to the road. If he ran up the next lot of steps, or the one after that, he could disappear completely before the others arrived. She crept down onto the towpath and started walking along behind him.

The next bridge was very long and dark—almost a

tunnel. Lizzie had to look down at her feet, to make sure she didn't trip, and when she looked up again Sam had vanished. She started running.

She burst out from under the bridge and almost fell over a pair of feet. They were Sam's and he was sitting on the bank beside the towpath, glowering at her.

'Go away,' he muttered. 'Stop following me.'

'I w-wasn't—' Lizzie stammered. 'I mean—'

Sam frowned. 'What are you up to? You don't even know who I am.'

'Yes I do.' Lizzie took a deep breath. 'You're Ethan's friend Sam. And you've run away from home.'

'So? That's none of your business! Get out of here! Leave me alone!'

Lizzie didn't want to make him angry, but how could she just walk away? She hesitated, not knowing what to do. And suddenly a voice called down from the top of the bridge.

'Lizzie!'

It was Ethan. He came racing down the steps and grabbed hold of Sam's arm.

'Let me go!' Sam yelled, trying to pull free.

'Don't be an idiot!' Ethan shouted. 'You can't run away just because of some stupid teacher! You mustn't—'

Sam glared at him, tugging harder, and suddenly he pulled himself free. But the effort made him lose his balance. He staggered backwards, over-balanced, and fell into the canal.

Lizzie leapt forward and caught hold of one of his

feet, which was all she could reach. 'Quick, Ethan!' she yelled. 'He's too heavy. I can't—'

For one terrible moment she thought she couldn't hang on. Then Ethan was there, pulling at one of Sam's arms. Together they hauled him out of the canal and dragged him backwards to lean against the bank on the other side of the towpath. He sat there, with water streaming down his face, looking utterly wretched.

Lizzie took off her coat and put it round his shoulders. 'We've got to get him somewhere warm. Phone his family, Ethan. Tell them to come and fetch him.'

'Leave me alone,' muttered Sam. 'Go away.'

Ethan crouched down suddenly, staring into Sam's face. 'Listen, you dodo. It's not just you! It's the *school*!'

Lizzie had no idea what he meant, but she saw Sam's expression change. He stopped glaring and looked puzzled.

'What are you talking about?' he said.

10

IT'S THE SCHOOL

'It's the school!' Ethan said again.

It came to him, suddenly, in a flash, when he saw how unhappy Sam was looking. *That's what Jatinder's face was like,* he thought. *When he opened the front door.* They both looked terrible.

Because they'd both been told they were rubbish at the thing they cared about most.

And they weren't the only ones . . . Ethan stared across the canal, working out how all the pieces fitted together.

'There's nothing wrong with your band,' he said. 'It's brilliant. Everyone thinks so. Mr Wilson said you were rubbish because . . . because something strange is happening. It's the school that's wrong, Sam, not the band.'

'The *school*?' Sam stared. 'What are you talking about?'

Lizzie didn't understand either. 'How can a school be wrong?'

Ethan shook his head. 'I don't know, but it is.' He looked at Sam. 'The band's your main thing. Right? Well, what's *Jatinder's* main thing?'

'IT, of course.' Sam shrugged. 'So?'

'So Mr Copeland's set him some impossible homework. Now Jatinder thinks he's rubbish at IT. And the History teacher gave Morgan some ancient document and told her she *had* to read it. Morgan *cried*.'

'*Morgan?*' Sam's mouth fell open. He nodded slowly, as if he'd just remembered something. 'Alex got a terrible mark for his Art project last week. It was fantastic, but Mrs Neal said a four-year-old could have done it better.'

Ethan nodded. 'I told you, there's something wrong with the school. It's started teaching people they can't do things.'

Sam frowned. 'But that's crazy. It's *evil*.'

'Your mum should complain,' Lizzie said.

Sam sat very still for a moment. Then he looked up—and his eyes were blazing. 'No—*we* ought to complain! All the kids in the school. We're the ones they're messing around with. We have to let them know they can't do that!'

At that moment, a car pulled up and stopped on the bridge. One of the doors banged and Jatinder appeared at the top of the steps. 'Thank goodness!' he said, when he saw Sam. He shouted back at the car. 'He's here!'

'It's your mum,' Ethan said, hoping Sam wasn't going to be angry. 'I told her you were here.'

Sam wasn't angry at all. He grinned and jumped up. 'Coming!' he called to Jatinder. He took off Lizzie's coat. 'Thanks for this. And for pulling me out of the canal.' He charged up the steps to the car, shouting, 'I need to get home fast! We have to call a meeting.'

In a couple of seconds, the car was pulling away from the kerb, leaving Ethan and Lizzie standing on the towpath.

'Wow,' Lizzie said. 'What a change. Is all that stuff true? About the terrible homework?'

Ethan nodded. 'Weird, isn't it?'

'I'm glad our school's not like that,' Lizzie said. 'Thank goodness we've got Ms Mountain. She makes everything so *exciting*.'

'What about your story?' Ethan remembered it suddenly. 'Did you have to stop writing to look for Sam?'

Lizzie shook her head. 'I was just sending it when I got your message.'

'You mean I've got it?' Ethan grinned at her. 'I'd better go home and read it.'

He meant to start reading as soon as he got home. But it wasn't that simple. Auntie Beryl was waiting for him, and she wasn't happy.

'Where have you been, Ethan Prendergast? You've been out *two and a half hours*.'

Ethan tried to explain, but he couldn't make her understand why Jatinder and Sam were upset.

'Children!' she sniffed. 'Always think you're smarter than everyone else. Teachers have to let you know you're not the best in the world.'

'But they shouldn't make you feel useless.' Ethan frowned. 'There's something wrong with that school. I know there is.'

'It was always fine when you were there,' Auntie Beryl said stubbornly.

Ethan didn't know how to convince her—until he checked his phone. There was an internet storm going on, with hundreds of posts from kids complaining about their teachers.

And all the kids were from Sam and Jatinder's school.

'Look,' he said. '*Look!*' He waved the phone under Auntie Beryl's nose. 'Read these. Then you'll see.'

She sat down at the kitchen table and put on her glasses. For a few seconds there was complete silence. Then she looked up at Ethan. 'Looks as though you're right,' she said slowly. 'There are *bad* things happening in that school. I always thought Mr Ramsey was a good Head, but I must have been wrong.'

'No, that's what's so strange,' Ethan said. 'Mr Ramsey *is* good—especially at encouraging people.'

Auntie Beryl frowned. 'Maybe he's gone. Maybe someone else is in charge.'

Ethan shook his head. 'Mr Ramsey's still there. I saw him going into that Mega Conference. He talked to me and he was really nice. The same as always.'

'So it's a mystery.' Auntie Beryl shrugged. 'Well, there's nothing we can do about it. You'd better get on with your homework.'

That was when Ethan remembered Lizzie's story. He nodded and jumped up. 'I'll go and start straight away.'

Running into his room, he opened up his laptop and found the email from Lizzie.

Here's my story. Is it OK? Can we talk tomorrow?

There was no time to waste. He opened the attachment, which was just called 'Story' and big, black letters spread across the screen:

The Mysterious Voice

Settling himself in his chair, Ethan sat back and started reading.

Way out in the middle of the ocean, a tiny island loomed through the mist. There were no houses on the island. There was just a small, orange tent, halfway up the mountain in the centre.

Outside the tent, two men and a woman huddled round a small campfire. It was night and they couldn't see anything beyond the light of the fire. Mist and darkness surrounded them.

Suddenly a noise drifted through the mist. A mysterious voice that seemed to come from all around them.

'I will obey all your instructions,' it said . . .

11

ANGELIKA LOSES
HER TEMPER

The next morning, as Lizzie and Tyler reached the school gates, there was a shout from behind them. Ethan cycled up and pulled in to the kerb.

'Hi!' he panted. 'Lizzie, your story—'

Tyler gave him a wave and walked on, into school, but Lizzie stopped and looked at Ethan. 'Have you read it? Is it OK?'

'I've read it *three times*!' Ethan grinned at her. 'It's fantastic. That creepy voice!' He shivered.

Now I can ask him about the video, Lizzie thought.

But she didn't get a chance to speak. Ethan was too keen to tell her his plans. He pushed his bike along beside her, talking very fast. 'I've got a fantastic idea for bringing the story to life. Nothing clunky. I just want to build on that eerie atmosphere. I'll record you reading the story and then—'

He started describing his ideas for images. She didn't understand half of what he said, but it sounded very exciting.

'I'll start work tonight,' Ethan said, as he wheeled his bike into the cycle shed. 'I mean—' he stopped and looked anxiously at Lizzie, 'if you like what I'm thinking.'

'It sounds great,' Lizzie said. 'But there's something I want to ask you.'

By then, they were inside the school, walking up the stairs to their classroom. Ethan nodded cheerfully. 'Ask away,' he said.

'Well, I wondered—'

But Lizzie never reached the end of her question. As they arrived at the top of the stairs, they heard an extraordinary noise coming from their classroom. Someone was shouting in an angry, outraged voice. On and on and on. Lizzie and Ethan looked at each other and then ran into the classroom.

It was Angelika. And she was furious. She was standing with a couple of other girls, shouting and waving her arms around, and when she saw Lizzie and Ethan, she ran up to them and started all over again.

'You know my friends—Hannah and Zainab? They did the dance workshop with me, at the Arts Explosion.'

'Those girls from your dancing school?' Lizzie said.

Angelika nodded. 'They both phoned me up last night, because they were *so upset* about what's happening at their school. Guess what Miss Davidson's done!'

'Miss Davidson?'

'She's the Head. And they've always said she was really lovely. But yesterday she sent an email round to all the parents, saying the school won't be doing Science any more. Or Sport. Or Maths or English or . . . or anything *normal*.'

'So what *are* they going to do?' Lizzie said.

Angelika looked as if she was going to explode.

'Fancy dress and paintballing!'

'WHAT???' Lizzie and Ethan shouted it together.

'Miss Davidson says all those old subjects are out of date and "children need to learn self-expression and self-assertion to fit them for the modern world".'

'So the fancy dress is self-expression?' said Ethan. 'And the paintballing is self-assertion?'

Angelika nodded. 'Hannah's frantic. If they don't do Science, how will she ever get to be a doctor? And how will Zainab cope without playing football? They've tried talking to Miss Davidson, but she just won't listen.'

'She'll have to listen,' Lizzie said. 'Or everyone's going to leave—'

'Leave what?' said a voice from the doorway.

It was Blake. He sauntered into the classroom and Angelika flew across to him and started explaining all over again. Her hands waved about, even more frantically, and she was almost too angry to speak.

Blake didn't get it at first. He thought she was joking and the angrier she got the more he laughed.

Lizzie could see there was going to be trouble. She went across and tried to make them both calm down, but they didn't even hear her. Angelika shouted louder and louder and Blake laughed more and more.

Until Blake said, 'But girls *love* fancy dress!'—and Angelika slapped him round the face.

Everything stopped then. There was a terrible silence. Blake put his hand up to his face and stared at Angelika, with his mouth open. She stared back—and then burst into tears.

Blake looked round at Lizzie and Ethan. 'I didn't think—I mean, all that stuff about paintballing and fancy dress instead of proper lessons—she wasn't *serious*, was she?'

'Oh, Blake,' Lizzie shook her head at him. 'You're an idiot. Couldn't you see how upset she was?'

Blake shuffled his feet. 'But it's stupid. No school's going to do something like that.'

'They *have*.' Angelika sniffed and wiped her eyes. 'I'm sorry I slapped you, Blake. But Hannah and Zainab are really upset. And so are their parents. They're getting together with lots of other parents, to organize a protest on Saturday. Outside the Town Hall.'

'A protest? You mean, like, a *march*?' Blake brightened. 'Hey, why don't we join in? I've always wanted to go on a protest march. We could have banners and everything. We might even get on TV.' He looked more and more excited. 'What time does it start?'

'Are you serious?' Angelika said. 'You really want to go on this protest?'

'Sure. Why not?' Blake beamed at Lizzie and Ethan. 'Why don't we *all* go? We could take Tyler and Robo too. We're sure to get on TV if we've got a robot with us. ROBOTS AGAINST PAINTBALLING. That would make a great banner.'

'I don't think they're against *paintballing*,' Ethan said. 'It's more—'

But Blake wasn't listening. He was too excited about the idea of going on a protest march. Before the others could calm him down, he went charging out into the corridor, telling everyone he saw that they had to come on the protest too.

Ethan looked at Lizzie. 'There's no way we can stop him. We'll have to go too, or he's bound to get into trouble.'

Lizzie sighed and nodded. And Angelika was nodding too. Much more vigorously.

'Of course we should go,' she said. 'Everyone ought to be protesting. I hope Miss Davidson turns up, so we can ask her what she's doing. It doesn't make sense. When Hannah started telling me, I thought it had to be someone else doing it—like one of the Deputy Heads. But Hannah said Miss Davidson was the one who wrote the letter. Which is totally *weird*. She's not that sort of Head at all.'

Ethan was suddenly very still. 'That makes *two* weird Heads,' he said slowly. 'Mr Ramsey—the Head at *my* old school—and now this one.'

But Angelika wasn't in any mood to listen. 'We can't worry about every school in town,' she said impatiently. 'It's Hannah and Zainab I care about. We need to help *them*—before their lives are ruined.'

'I didn't want to stop you,' Ethan said. 'I just thought—'

Before he could finish, Miss Wellington came marching into the room, chivvying Blake along in front of her.

'I don't care *what* you're doing on Saturday,' she was saying. 'What you should be doing today is sitting in here, ready for registration. *Without talking.*'

Blake looked stubborn. 'I only—'

'Silence!' thundered Miss Wellington. 'Go and sit down!'

Blake went to his place, but he couldn't keep still. He sat there scribbling notes and flicking them across to other people. PROTEST SATURDAY, said the one that landed in front of Lizzie. BE THERE!!!

He and Angelika spent the rest of the day talking about the protest. Lizzie kept trying to calm them down, so they didn't get into trouble. It was so hard that she actually forgot about her story for the rest of the day.

12

FINDING THE
MYSTERIOUS VOICE

But Ethan hadn't forgotten. He kept thinking about it, and especially about the mysterious voice. That was the key to a great presentation. Lizzie should read the rest of the story, but the mysterious voice ought to be computer-generated.

Could he do it? Could he create an eerie, frightening voice? Something that would grab people's attention from the very beginning, when it sounded across the island as the explorers arrived:

I will obey all your instructions.

Right up to the end, when all three of the explorers were lying dead on the mountain and the voice rang out for the last time:

I have obeyed all your instructions.

He knew he could produce some fantastic graphics—especially if Jatinder helped him—but he didn't know how to generate the voice. Could he use some kind of filter . . .?

He started as soon as he got home, but he still hadn't solved the problem when Auntie Beryl said it was time for bed.

'I just need a little bit longer—'

Auntie Beryl wouldn't even listen. She stood over him until he turned off his laptop, and then chased him into the bathroom. 'You're a growing boy. You *need* sleep.'

Maybe she was right, but it was no use sending him to bed. He *couldn't* sleep. He kept going over and over the same question. How could he create the right voice for Lizzie's story? He was still trying to work it out when he heard Auntie Beryl going to bed.

And then, just as he was starting to get drowsy, he thought of a solution. It came to him in a flash—and he was desperate to know if it would work. Creeping out of bed, he opened his laptop and started again.

He woke up in the morning with a pain in his cheek and a furious voice ranting in his ear.

'Ethan Prendergast, *what do you think you're doing?*'

'I—er—' He blinked and lifted his face off the keyboard.

Auntie Beryl was standing over him, glowering at the computer. 'Have you been on that thing all night? What were you *doing?*'

'It's—something I promised to do for Lizzie. Do you want to see?' Ethan shuffled the mouse, to wake up the computer.

'I do *not* want to see.' Auntie Beryl shook her head crossly. 'You need to have your shower and get dressed.

Breakfast's almost ready.'

'But it's the weekend. Can't I have breakfast in my pyjamas?'

Auntie Beryl sniffed. 'It's Saturday, not Sloppyday. You've got five minutes.'

Ethan had the quickest shower in the history of the universe. He cleaned his teeth, dressed, and skidded into the kitchen. Auntie Beryl looked at her watch.

'Four minutes and fifty-eight seconds. Good. Do you want one bagel or two?'

'Two, please. Can Lizzie come over after breakfast? We're working together and there's something I need to show her.'

Before he fell asleep, he'd found the perfect voice. And he wanted to see Lizzie's face when she heard it.

By half past ten, Lizzie was there, and Ethan's hand was hovering over the mouse.

'You have to tell me,' he said, 'if you don't think it's right.'

Lizzie nodded, without taking her eyes off the screen, and Ethan started his video. Slowly, the map of an island swam into focus, in the middle of a misty grey screen. After a second, the centre of the island began to shimmer and shift. Pale words formed across it, spelling out the title of the story.

The Mysterious Voice.

And then the voice spoke. It was cold and impersonal, pitched midway between a man's voice and a woman's. Not quite mechanical, but somehow . . . not quite human either.

I will obey all your instructions.

Lizzie took a long, slow breath, staring at the screen. 'Yes,' she murmured. 'That's *just* what it was like.'

'What?' Ethan stopped the video. 'You mean it was a *real* voice?'

Lizzie nodded, without looking at him. 'I heard it coming from inside one of the tents, at the Arts Explosion.'

'Whose voice was it?'

'I don't know. It was like the voice in your video, but it was . . . kind of familiar too. Familiar, but *wrong*.'

Ethan tried to imagine that. 'You couldn't work out who it was?'

Lizzie shook her head. 'I looked on that film Robo took. It shows someone coming out of that tent, but the picture's too small to see properly.'

'Couldn't you zoom in?'

'That just turned it into a blur.'

'Let's have a go.' Ethan reached for the mouse. 'I've got the film on here, but I haven't had a chance to look at it yet. Hang on.' He found it and started fast-forwarding. 'Tell me when to stop.'

But it was Ethan who stopped the film. When he spotted a black car sliding in through the school gates.

'Hey! That's the car that almost knocked me over!' He zoomed in for a better view.

'You mean the posh car?' Lizzie leaned forward to look. 'What's that thing on the side?'

'Some kind of symbol, I think.' Ethan zoomed in on the round, golden shape. 'Looks like a picture of the globe. With some words underneath it.'

'New—New something.' Lizzie leaned in closer, peering at the letters. *New World Education Consultants.* She frowned. 'What does that mean?'

'Don't know. But it was at the Mega Conference. And it looks like the same driver.' Ethan started the film again. 'Yes, there he is, getting out. And there's someone in the back too.'

The red-haired driver went round to the far side of the car and opened the back door, to let his passenger out. There was a quick glimpse of someone in dark clothes—someone tall, with very pale hair—and then Robo must have turned away, because the camera panned back to the field.

'Who was *that*?' Ethan said.

13

THE FIGURE IN
THE RED DRESS

Who cared who it was? Lizzie couldn't see why Ethan was fussing over a car. She wanted to get on with finding the person coming out of that little tent.

'It's further on,' she said. 'That bit we're looking for.'

'What? Oh, yes.' Ethan blinked, as if he'd almost forgotten about the voice. He set the video running again.

Lizzie leaned forward, watching the field clear as people went into their workshops. It couldn't be much longer. Just a few seconds . . .

And there it was! 'Stop! That's me, walking between those two tents.'

Ethan stopped the film again. 'So you're hearing the voice? Just at that moment?'

Lizzie nodded. 'Then I come out from between the tents and go back to my workshop. And *then*—'

'Then the mysterious voice person comes out of that little tent. Right?' Ethan went on a few frames. And there was the little figure Lizzie had seen before. The red blob coming out of the tent.

'Can you make that any clearer?' she said.

'I'll have a go.'

Ethan started editing the picture. He zoomed in and sharpened it and changed the colours—and did other things Lizzie didn't understand. But it was no use. Whatever he tried, there was nothing to see except a fuzzy shape.

He shook his head. 'Sorry. It's just someone in a red dress. Like—' He stopped suddenly.

'Like what?' Lizzie looked at him, but he didn't meet her eyes. He was gazing at the screen again.

'Like Ms Mountain,' he said, in a slow, puzzled voice. '*She* was wearing a red dress, wasn't she? But it couldn't have been her. Could it?'

'No!' Lizzie said quickly. 'Of course it couldn't!' Suddenly she felt very peculiar. Because maybe the mysterious voice *had* been a bit like . . . just a *little* bit like . . .

But that must be a coincidence. *Of course* it wasn't Ms Mountain. She stood up and started putting her coat on.

'Where are you going?' Ethan said. 'You can't leave yet. I need to record you reading the story.'

Lizzie shook her head. She didn't want to stay and talk about that picture. 'I've got to get home. We're having lunch early, because Mum's got a hospital appointment. And Tyler and I are going to the protest. Aren't you coming too?'

Ethan blinked. It looked as though he'd forgotten about it. 'Um . . . yes, of course,' he muttered as they went towards the front door.

Lizzie nodded. 'OK. See you this afternoon!'

As she opened the front door, Auntie Beryl came out of the kitchen. 'What's going on this afternoon, then?'

'The protest,' Lizzie said. 'At the Town Hall.'

'You're not going on *that*!' Auntie Beryl shook her head at Ethan, looking horrified.

'Why not?' Ethan said. 'It's only going to be a few parents complaining about a school.'

'Not *one* school!' Auntie Beryl said. 'Haven't you seen the local news? It's not just Lane Road School that's being ruined. At Marshal Street, they've sacked the cleaners and invented a subject called *Domestic Hygiene*—which means the children have to clean the school. The Head at Symington School says the parents have to come in and take the same exams as their children. And at Cuthbert Junior they're having all their lessons in the swimming pool. There'll be parents from all those schools going to the protest!'

And from Sam and Jatinder's school too, Lizzie thought. *It's going to be huge.*

'We promised we'd go,' Ethan said. 'To help Angelika's friends.'

Auntie Beryl frowned. 'Well, you'll have to break your promise. And Lizzie's parents won't let her go either, if they've got any sense.' She folded her arms, in a way that meant, *This discussion is finished.*

Lizzie hurried home, feeling embarrassed. Was Ethan's aunt right? Would her mum and dad stop her going to the protest?

At first, it looked like that. All through lunch, her dad tried to persuade them not to do it. 'Crowds can be dangerous,' he said.

Mrs Warren shook her head sadly. 'And Tyler's not very tall. People will push you around, Tyler.'

'I'll have Lizzie,' Tyler said. 'And Robo. He would never let anyone hurt me.'

Mr Warren shook his head impatiently, but Mrs Warren looked thoughtful. 'Actually, that's a good point,' she said. 'No one's going to push Robo out of the way. Everyone loves robots.'

'Everyone loves *Robo*!' Tyler gave the robot a hug. 'He'll look after me—and Lizzie as well.'

Their dad nodded slowly. 'I guess you're right. Having Robo there will keep you safe—and he might even get you on the news.' He grinned. 'If there are reporters at the protest, they're bound to notice a robot.'

'That would be good!' Mrs Warren said. 'The more publicity the better. We *have* to stop our schools being wrecked! I wish you and I could go on the protest too.'

Mr Warren patted her hand. 'You mustn't miss your hospital appointment.'

'Of course you mustn't.' Lizzie gave her mum a hug. 'You go to the hospital—and we'll tell you all about the protest when you get back.'

14

NEW WORLD

Nothing would make Auntie Beryl change her mind. In the end, Ethan gave up and sent Lizzie a message. Sorry I can't come.

Lizzie's reply came straight back. Don't worry. Still 4 of us to keep Blake out of trouble.

Ethan was puzzled. 4???

Robo of course!

Oh, great. Even *robots* were going. Everyone would be at the protest—except him. Thanks, Auntie Beryl. Oh well, at least he could get on with Lizzie's presentation.

He was just about to start, when he remembered Sam and Jatinder. Would they be on the protest too? He sent them both a quick message.

How are things going?

Sam replied straight away. I think we're winning! Check out the local news!!

Ethan did. It wasn't hard to find. The story was right at the top of the local news page:

A New World for Lane Road School?

The governors of troubled Lane Road School are seeking advice from educational consultants New World. Pupils at Lane Road have repeatedly been

given work beyond their abilities There are reports of children suffering from depression and running away from home.

Simon Weatherby, New World's Chief Executive, says, 'New World believes in helping all students to progress at the right pace.'

There is no comment from Mr Ramsey, Lane Road's Head Teacher.

New World again! But it wasn't the report that made Ethan stare. It was the picture beside it—a photo of a short man with red curly hair standing next to a large black car with a golden globe painted on its side. The caption underneath the photo said: *New World boss, Simon Weatherby.*

Suddenly, that red-haired man was everywhere. At the Arts Explosion. At the Mega Conference. And now he was talking to the governors at Lane Road. What was going on?

Who were these New World people? Ethan had a look for their website, but he couldn't find one. There was no information at all on the internet. He was going to give up, when he remembered Robo's video. Maybe he'd take another look at those pictures of the car . . .

He ran them through, frame by frame, studying each one. The driver was Simon Weatherby all right. But he didn't look like the *boss* of anything. From the way he went round to open the door for his passenger, he looked more like a kind of chauffeur.

So who *was* the passenger in the back of the car?

He only appeared in the last two or three frames. Ethan enlarged those, as much as he could, and studied them carefully. The man's face was hidden, but he was obviously tall. And his hair was very pale. As he stared at the blurred pictures, Ethan found himself shivering.

A tall man, with very pale fair hair . . .

Was it possible . . .? For a moment, he almost stopped breathing. *Come on!* he told himself. *There must be millions of tall, fair-haired men in the world. Of course it's not the Headmaster.*

But suppose it was? Suppose the Headmaster was back? Ethan stared at the screen, with his heart thumping. There were lots of peculiar things happening. Some of the Heads who had been at the Mega Conference were behaving in very strange ways. And Simon Weatherby hadn't been the only person in the New World car that day. *Someone else* had been sitting in the back.

Was it a tall man? With very pale fair hair . . .?

Ethan looked at those pictures for a long time. Then he sent the clearest one to Lizzie.

Remind you of anyone?

15

THE PROTEST

Lizzie didn't hear the picture arrive. She and Tyler were just walking into the Town Hall Square and it was impossible to hear anything except the sound of shouting. The Square was jammed full of people, all shouting and waving banners.

NO FANCY DRESS! NO PAINTBALLING!
DOWN WITH SCHOOL IN THE SWIMMING POOL!
STOP EXAMS FOR PARENTS!
MR RAMSEY MUST RESIGN!

The crowd was even bigger than Lizzie had expected. She couldn't see Blake or Angelika anywhere. And even if she did find out where they were, she and Tyler would never be able to reach them. Was there any point in staying? No one would notice whether they were there or not. There seemed to be someone up on the Town Hall steps, making a speech, but she couldn't hear a word. And it was hard to see anything except the backs of the people in front of her.

She tugged at Tyler's sleeve. *Let's go home*, she was going to say. But, before she could get the words out, something strange started happening. The man in front of them glanced over his shoulder and saw Robo. He turned back, to nudge the woman next to him, and she looked round and then whispered to the two people in front of her. Then *they* looked back . . .

It was like a ripple running through the crowd. Until that moment, everyone had been facing forwards, gazing up at the Town Hall steps. But now people were turning to look at Robo. They were muttering and pointing and some them were shuffling back, to leave a way through.

'What shall I do?' Tyler whispered in Lizzie's ear.

'Go for it!' she whispered back. 'Come on!'

She gave Tyler a little push and he and Robo started moving through the crowd, with Lizzie close behind them. People stepped out of their way, as if they had a magic pass.

And then the cheering started.

'Go, Robot!' yelled two women with a buggy.

'Great to see you!' bellowed a man with a banner saying MISS DAVIDSON MUST GO!!!!!!

'Give the robot a placard!' someone shouted. 'Get it up there at the front. Beside the speakers!'

Lizzie kept looking for Blake and Angelika, but she couldn't see them. And there was no time to stop. She had to make sure she didn't lose Tyler and Robo.

Robo was the important one. There was no doubt about that. People were stepping back to let him through and waving him to the front. He had almost reached the steps at the front of the Town Hall, when Lizzie finally caught sight of Angelika. She waved frantically, and

Angelika waved back and wriggled through the crowd to join them.

'I never thought it would be like this!' she panted. 'I didn't think I'd *ever* find you. Have you seen Blake?'

Lizzie shook her head. 'I haven't even *heard* him.'

She was holding on to Tyler's arm, very tightly, but she couldn't do anything about Robo. Dozens of hands reached out to seize him, pulling him away from Tyler and hoisting him up to the top of the steps.

'Hey!' Tyler shouted. 'That's my robot!'

He tried to follow, but Angelika grabbed his other hand and helped Lizzie hold him back. 'It's OK,' she said, into Tyler's ear. 'They won't hurt him. They think he's great.'

At the top of the steps, there was a man with a microphone, making a speech. He wasn't put off when a robot suddenly appeared beside him. Waving a hand at Robo, he worked him into the speech.

'*That's* how Mr Ramsey sees the children at Lane Road!' he bellowed. 'Like robots, just waiting to be programmed! Never needing rest or exercise—or *fun*! We have to stop him ruining their school!'

Huge, angry roars went up from the crowd. 'YES!!!'

'Save OUR children's school too!'

'Get rid of all the rubbish Heads!'

Lizzie shivered, but the roars made Tyler even more excited. Pulling his hands free, he jumped up beside Robo and waved at the crowd.

'No!' Lizzie shouted. 'Come back, Ty!'

'Don't worry about him,' Angelika said. 'He's loving it.'

'But everyone's taking photos!' Lizzie wailed. 'What will Mum and Dad say?'

Tyler called down to them. 'Robo's going to be famous! He's going to be on the news!'

Lizzie was frantic. 'That's my brother!' she shouted up at the man with the microphone. 'Make him come down! There's nothing wrong with our school. We're at Hazelbrook!'

That just made things worse. The speaker waved an arm at Tyler and bellowed into his microphone. 'This boy—this sensible, brave boy—has no complaints about his own school. *But he's come out to support us!* Even children can see that what's happening is WRONG! We must get rid of the rogue Heads!'

'YES!' yelled the crowd. 'Out! Out! OUT!'

'Let's MARCH!' yelled the man with the microphone.

Running down the steps, he charged towards the road leading out of the Square. The crowd streamed after him, shouting and waving placards. Lizzie caught hold of Tyler's jacket and held him back.

'Quick!' she shouted to Angelika. 'Get Robo—before someone takes him off on the march!'

Angelika ran up the steps and flung her arms round the robot, clinging on to him as people tried to carry him off.

'His . . . his battery's flat,' she shouted. 'He needs recharging.'

It wasn't true, but it worked. The crowd streamed past, leaving them behind. Tyler wanted to go too, and he was complaining loudly, but Lizzie could see

Angelika keeping a tight hold on to Robo. She knew Tyler wouldn't go off without him.

They didn't see Blake until the crowd had almost disappeared. He was right at the back of the march, waving a banner and chanting, 'Heads—OUT!' with a huge smile all over his face.

'He's *enjoying* it,' Angelika said, in a disgusted voice. 'As if it's some kind of party.' She glowered at Blake's back as he vanished up the road.

Lizzie was watching Blake as well. 'Should we go after him?' she said. 'So he doesn't get into trouble?'

Tyler pulled a face. 'He won't listen to us. He doesn't care about trouble.'

Angelika nodded. 'No, he doesn't. But I know what he *does* care about. Hang on.' She felt in her pocket, and pulled out some change. 'Send him a message, Liz, while I nip across to that shop.'

'What message?' Lizzie said. 'What are we doing?'

Angelika grinned. 'Tell him we're all having cake in the park. He won't miss out on that.'

Lizzie laughed. 'You'd better hurry, or he'll be there before us. And he'll be really angry if there isn't any cake.'

They just made it. They reached the bandstand— with a big bag of flapjacks—two minutes before Blake came charging through the park gates. He was so excited that he couldn't stop talking.

'Wasn't it great? There were hundreds of people there! *Thousands!* And the television cameras were filming *everything*! The television people were going to interview *me*—but then they said it wasn't any use because my school is OK, but it was really exciting talking to the reporter and—poor old Ethan, missing it all—'

Angelika gave him three flapjacks at once and he stopped talking. But Lizzie kept thinking about the television cameras. Suppose Tyler and Robo were on the news. Suppose they *all* were. Would Ethan feel left out?

'Come back to our house,' she said. 'I'll see if Ethan wants to come too.'

'Great idea!' Blake beamed at her. 'Then we can watch ourselves on the news!'

'You really think you'll be on the news?' Angelika said scornfully. 'Your face would break everyone's TV screen.'

'Bet you we are,' Tyler said. 'Robo's bound to be on.' He patted the robot's arm. 'Come on, let's go!'

Lizzie pulled out her phone to send Ethan a message—and stopped, staring down at the picture he'd sent her. It was a blurry close-up of a tall man getting out of a car.

A tall man in black clothes, with very pale fair hair.

The Headmaster, said her brain. *It's like the Headmaster*.

For a second, she froze, unable to move. Unable to drag her eyes away from the picture that *couldn't* be, that *mustn't* be . . .

Then Tyler turned round. 'What's that you're looking at?' he said.

'Nothing! Just a silly picture.' Lizzie turned off her phone, as fast as she could, and pushed her phone deep into her pocket. Tyler mustn't see that photo. It would give him nightmares. And all for nothing.

Because it *wasn't* the Headmaster. It *couldn't* be.

16

ON TV

Ethan cycled straight round to Lizzie's flat, the moment he got her message. He was looking forward to hearing about the protest, but what he really wanted was a chance to talk to Lizzie on her own. About that picture.

It wasn't going to be easy, though. He saw that as soon as he walked into the flat.

'It's a bit of a squash,' Lizzie said, as she let him in. 'But I've saved you a cushion.'

Everyone was crammed into the Warrens' little sitting room. Lizzie's mum was on the sofa, propped up with pillows, Lizzie's dad and Blake (of course!) were in the armchairs, and all the others were on the floor.

Blake was so busy talking that he didn't notice Ethan at first. 'I was right up at the front,' he was saying. 'Really close to the Town Hall steps. *And* I went to the school after that. It was *fantastic*! Better than going to the football! There were all these people and banners and—just wait till you see it on the news!'

'It might not be on,' said Lizzie's mum.

'Of course it will,' Blake said. 'It was a HUGE protest. Quick! Turn on the TV.' The local news was just about to begin and, as it started, he punched the air triumphantly. 'Yay! I was right!'

'SSHH!' said everyone else.

But he *was* right. The protest was the lead story on the local news. As the pictures came up, Lizzie's dad grinned and ruffled Tyler's hair.

'There you are, Ty. You look as if you're going to make a speech.'

'It was Robo they wanted,' Blake said. 'Everyone thought he was fantastic and he should have come to the school too, but his battery was flat and he couldn't so—'

Angelika put her hand over his mouth.

The picture on the screen changed. Now the crowd wasn't outside the Town Hall. It was in front of a school, and people were yelling and shaking the gates.

'What's the point of that?' Lizzie's mum shuddered. 'It's no use shouting slogans at the building. They ought to be talking to the Head. What's *she* got to say about all this?'

As if the television had heard her, the picture changed again, to show a man sitting at an untidy desk.

'That's Mr Ramsey!' Ethan said. 'But why does he look—?'

'Sshh!' hissed everyone else.

Mr Ramsey stared out of the screen with a strange, glazed expression on his face. 'Parents know nothing about education,' he said, in a cold voice. 'This is *my* school and I shall run it in my own way.'

Lizzie's dad glowered at the screen. 'That man should lose his job! Straight away!'

'But—' Ethan didn't understand. 'Mr Ramsey's not like that.'

Lizzie's mother shook her head sadly. 'You heard him.'

Before Ethan could answer, Mr Ramsey disappeared from the screen.

'That interview was recorded an hour ago,' the newsreader said. 'We understand that, since then, Mr Ramsey has resigned. So have at least three other Head Teachers.' She turned to the man sitting next to her. 'Simon Weatherby, you run an education consultancy service. What do *you* think about the situation in these schools?'

And there he was *again*. Ethan could hardly believe it. Simon Weatherby from New World, with his round face and his curly red hair.

'Schools are machines for learning,' Simon Weatherby said, in a crisp, unemotional voice. 'They should be producing the workers our country needs. But these schools are broken machines. No wonder the parents are calling for change.'

The newsreader nodded wisely. 'Can you see a way to bring that change about?'

'I can.' Simon Weatherby gave her a brisk smile. 'New World offers order and efficiency. Several schools have already called us in and we expect more to follow when they see what we achieve. All our schools are excellent education machines.'

'*Machines?*' Lizzie's mum shuddered again. 'How dreadful!' She reached for the remote and switched the TV off.

'No, he's right,' Lizzie's dad said. 'Schools need

someone sensible to sort them out. Someone with a *plan.*'

'Hazelbrook doesn't!' Tyler said fiercely. 'It's a great school! *We've* got Ms Mountain—and the Amazing Island Experience!'

'Oh, I'm not worried about *Hazelbrook,*' Mr Warren said. 'It's absolutely—'

They never discovered what he was going to say, because Blake suddenly looked at his watch and yelped. 'I've got to get home and video my drum solo! It has to reach Ms Mountain by midnight tomorrow! And we haven't planned the snacks yet.' He grabbed Angelika's hand and dragged her onto her feet.

Angelika pulled a face. 'OK—but only if we plan the snacks first. I'm not listening to you bashing the drums for hours and hours.'

'I have to do my video too!' Tyler jumped to his feet. 'I need to borrow the saw, Dad.'

'Only if I can keep an eye on you.' Mr Warren nodded to Ethan and Lizzie. 'What about you two? Haven't you got a video to make?'

'I have to record Lizzie reading her story.' Ethan looked across at her. 'I've brought my laptop, so we could do it outside. How about the park? It's really quiet over there.' *And I can ask you about that picture—and the Headmaster.*

Lizzie gave him a sharp look, as if she knew what he was thinking. She didn't speak until they were outside the flat. Then she said, 'This isn't about my story, is it? It's about that photo you sent.'

Ethan nodded. 'What do you think?'

'It's . . .' Lizzie hesitated. 'OK, it's a *bit* like the Headmaster. But how can it be him?'

'Why not?' Ethan said. 'Look at all the weird things going on in schools.'

Lizzie shook her head. 'They're not the kind of things the Headmaster would do. He likes *order*. Why would he tell kids to go paintballing? Or have their lessons in a swimming pool?'

'Maybe he's trying to wreck those schools, so he can take over. If he was at Ms Mountain's Mega Conference—'

'Why would she ask him to do that?'

'Maybe he hypnotized her. Maybe the mysterious voice—'

'No,' Lizzie said sharply. 'It's got nothing to do with Ms Mountain. She's never met the Headmaster—so how could he have hypnotized her? Now, are we going to record my story?'

It was like watching a shutter come down. Lizzie *really* didn't want to talk about the Headmaster. Ethan could see that. She couldn't bear the idea he had anything to do with Ms Mountain.

Ethan didn't like the idea either, but he had to think it through. Lizzie was right about one thing. There was no proof Ms Mountain had met the Headmaster. And nothing weird was happening at Hazelbrook. So maybe he was wrong about the mysterious voice . . .

He turned through the gate into the park. 'Come on then, let's get on with the recording. There won't be any traffic noise if we go over by the bandstand. We might get the sound of the wind in the bushes—but that would be great.'

17

THE LUCKY FIVE

As soon as they'd finished the recording, Ethan went home. Lizzie didn't hear any more from him until a message came on Sunday evening:

Phew! Finished at last! Couldn't get hold of Jatinder, so I had to do it all myself. Here's the link. Have a look and tell me if it's OK to send to Ms M.

Lizzie followed the link, with her heart thundering against her ribs. The video *had* to be OK. It was up against Tyler sawing Robo in half. And Blake crashing away on the drums while people munched Angelika's cupcakes. Suppose it was no good?

She sat back in her chair and watched the island come into focus. And then the words of the title spreading across it . . .

The Mysterious Voice . . .

It was perfect, from the very first seconds to the final shots, when it pulled away from the island—as if the camera was rising into the air—to show the bodies of the three murdered explorers. With the mysterious voice sounding again:

I have obeyed all your instructions.

For the first time, Lizzie let herself hope she might be one of the lucky five. Would Ms Mountain choose her? Was it possible . . .?

She was so excited that she didn't sleep very much. But even though she was tired, she jumped out of bed on Monday morning. And she hardly heard Tyler's chatter as they walked to school.

'Do you think I'll get picked, Lizzie? Dad said my video was brilliant, but it's only one trick really. Will Ms Mountain think that's boring . . .?'

He went on and on and on. Lizzie kept saying, 'I thought it was very good,' and 'I'm sure it will be OK,' but she wasn't really listening. All they could do was wait and see.

The whole school was electric with excitement. Everyone wanted to see the winning videos—and find out who was going to the island. But it wasn't going to happen that day. The big screen outside the hall said:

Ms Mountain is watching your videos—Not long to wait!

There was no sign of her on Monday. Or Tuesday, or Wednesday, or Thursday. That meant four days when Lizzie couldn't concentrate on anything. And four more nights when she couldn't sleep. By Friday morning, she could hardly keep her eyes open . . .

. . . until she walked into school and saw that the message on the big screen had changed. Now, there were huge, multi-coloured letters splashed across it:

IT'S TODAY!!!

Suddenly, she was very wide awake. Ethan grinned at her, but she was too nervous to grin back. This was it. The day they were going to find out.

Straight after registration, they went into the hall, and there was Ms Mountain beaming down at them. The last people were still taking their places when she started talking.

'I have seen SO MANY AMAZING VIDEOS since midnight on Sunday! You're brilliant, all of you, and it's been really tough picking the winners. But I've done it! Are you ready to see the top five?'

Voices roared from all over the hall. 'YES!'

'Here we go then. Get ready for lots of noise!'

She was right. The first video was Blake's drum solo—and it was *very* loud. His drumsticks moved so fast Lizzie could hardly see them, until he finished with a last crash of the cymbals and looked straight into the camera. 'OK, everyone,' he said. 'Time for refreshments!'

And suddenly there was Angelika, with a trolley, not on the video, but in real life. She wheeled it down the centre of the hall, handing out baskets full of tiny cupcakes.

As people munched, Ms Mountain introduced the next video. 'I'm not sure I understand everything on this one,' she said. 'But I've had it checked out by a mathematician and he tells me it's brilliant.'

'Must be Conan O'Dell's,' Ethan whispered. 'No one else is that good at Maths.'

He was right. The video was full of charts and tables, each one dissolving into the next while Conan's voice explained what was going on. Lizzie was sure no one in the hall understood it, except Conan and the Maths teachers, but she kept her eyes fixed on the screen, trying to shut out the little voice in her head, *That's two places gone,* it kept saying. *Only three left now.*

There was polite applause at the end of Conan's video, with some people grumbling under their breath, because they thought their own were better.

'And now for something *completely* different,' Ms Mountain said cheerfully. 'I hope no one's squeamish . . .'

Conan and his Maths presentation vanished—and someone else appeared. Someone quite small, with a big, shiny saw in his hand—

'Yay! It's me!' yelled Tyler, from three rows in front of Lizzie. 'I'M GOING TO THE ISLAND!!!'

Everyone started laughing and clapping as Robo joined Tyler on the screen, carrying a long box on his outstretched metal arms. He put the box down and took off the lid.

'Into the box, Robo!' ordered Tyler's voice. The robot climbed in and lay down, with his feet sticking out at one end of the box and his head at the other. Tyler fixed on the lid and then picked up a huge, gleaming saw.

Lizzie had seen the trick dozens of times, but she had to admit it looked great on the screen. There was a gasp when Tyler slid the two halves of the box apart, showing what looked like gears and circuit boards in the middle of Robo's body.

'That's neat,' Ethan muttered in Lizzie's ear. 'Well done, Ty.'

But the video hadn't finished. When Robo was safely back on his metal feet—all in one piece—Tyler handed him the saw and climbed into the box himself. His head was facing the audience and he pulled an agonized face when Robo started sawing. Even Lizzie was laughing.

At the end of the presentation, Tyler and Robo stood side by side in front of the box, taking a bow. The applause was like thunder and Ms Mountain had to hold up her hand for silence.

'So now *four* places are filled,' she said, when the hall was quiet.

Four? Lizzie looked at Ethan. How was that possible? They had only seen three videos.

Ms Mountain grinned and held up four fingers, counting off the names. 'Blake Vinney, Conan O'Dell, Tyler Warren and—Robo the robot.'

There was another roar of delight and a yell of triumph from Tyler. 'I told you, Lizzie! I *told* you Robo was going!'

Now there was only one place left. Lizzie could see most people had given up hope of going to the island. They were laughing and munching cake as they waited for the last video. Lizzie felt more like bursting into tears.

Ms Mountain waited for silence. Then she signalled to Mr Carson to play the last video. Lizzie wasn't sure she could bear to watch it. She clenched her hands together and closed her eyes. *I'm not going to cry. I'm NOT.*

Everyone in the hall was suddenly very still. Lizzie thought they were waiting for the video to start. But then, sliding into the silence, came a voice that was almost too soft to hear. A cold, impersonal voice, pitched midway between a man's and a woman's. And somehow . . . not quite human.

I will obey all your instructions.

Then she heard her own voice, beginning to tell the story.

When the video finished, there was complete silence for a moment. Then everyone in the hall started clapping and cheering.

Angelika leaned over to whisper in Lizzie's ear. 'That was *so frightening*! How did you get the idea?'

'Tell you later,' Lizzie whispered back. She was staring up at the stage, still not quite able to believe that she was one of Them. The five lucky ones. She was going to the island!

Ms Mountain looked down from the stage, letting them all cheer for a moment. Then she held up her hand for silence. 'Well done *everyone*,' she said. 'But especially to the winners; Blake Vinney, Conan O'Dell, Lizzie Warren, Tyler Warren—and Robo. Your videos are amazing and I know we're going to have a fantastic time together. Are you ready for the trip?'

Tyler jumped up, waving his arms. 'Yes!' he shouted.

'Yes, yes, YES!'

Ms Mountain beamed down at him. 'Well, I'm ready too. I just need to contact your parents, to tell them all the arrangements. I'll have to do that today, because we're leaving—' she stopped and looked round, 'we're leaving on *Monday*.'

Lizzie gasped. That was much sooner than she'd expected. Could she and Tyler be ready in time?

Tyler obviously didn't care about that. He was so excited he was bouncing up and down in his chair. Ms Mountain looked up at the clock.

'Let's have break now,' she said. 'I can see one person who needs to run off some excitement. You can all go outside for twenty minutes.'

That was just what Tyler needed. When Lizzie arrived outside, with Ethan and Angelika, Tyler was running round and round the football pitch.

'We won!' he was shouting. 'We won! We're going to the island! Suc-ces-sors! Suc-ces-sors! SUC-CES-SORS!'

18

SUCCESSORS!

'What's he talking about?' Angelika said. 'Successors to what?'

'Let's ask him,' Ethan said. The next time Tyler ran past, he reached out and caught him by the arm. 'Hang on, Ty. What's that you're shouting?'

Tyler gave a huge grin and shouted it again. 'We're the SUCCESSORS!'

'That doesn't mean anything,' Angelika said.

'Yes, it does.' Tyler looked at her as though she was stupid. 'Robo and I are going to the island. We've succeeded—and everyone else is a loser.'

'Don't be mean,' Lizzie said sharply. 'And anyway, *successor* doesn't mean that.'

'It doesn't?' Tyler frowned.

'It means . . . it means . . .' Lizzie looked round at Angelika. 'How can I explain?'

'It's like . . . you know . . . when a king dies,' Angelika said. 'The one who comes after him is his *successor*.'

Tyler pulled a face. 'That doesn't make sense. Ms Mountain's not a king.'

'What's it got to do with Ms Mountain?' Ethan said.

Tyler shook his head, as if they were all being stupid. 'It was *her* DVD, of course. That said *To my successor*.'

He raced off again, still shouting 'Successors!'

Ethan stared after him, with his mouth falling open.

'What's the matter?' said Angelika.

'That DVD,' Ethan said. 'It fell out of Ms Mountain's handbag, the first day she was here. Remember? Tyler ran after her, to give it back. He told us it said *To my—my*—something about success.'

'So?' Lizzie didn't get it.

'It must have been *To my successor*,' Ethan said. 'Tyler didn't know the word and he guessed what it meant.'

'So?' Angelika said impatiently.

'So who would call Ms Mountain *My successor*?' Ethan didn't understand why they couldn't see. 'It must have been from the *Headmaster*!'

Lizzie's eyes opened very wide. 'You think he left a DVD for the next Head to find?'

'Why would he do that?' Angelika said scornfully.

'So he could hypnotize her, of course.' Ethan was getting impatient. 'I bet that's what was on the DVD. A video of the Headmaster saying, *Look into my eyes . . .*'

Angelika sniffed. 'Well, it didn't work, did it? Ms Mountain's the *opposite* of the Headmaster. He would hate everything she does.' She shook her head and went off to the drinks machine.

Ethan looked at Lizzie. 'Do you think it's rubbish too?'

Lizzie hesitated. 'We-ell . . .'

'It all fits,' Ethan said urgently. '*Think!* The passenger in the New World car *was* the Headmaster. I'm sure it was. And the person with the mysterious voice—that *was* Ms Mountain. The Headmaster's back, Lizzie. We have to find out what he's planning.'

Lizzie looked down at her feet. 'OK, the mysterious voice *could* have been Ms Mountain. But if the Headmaster's hypnotized her, why isn't he doing anything?'

'He's not doing anything *here*. But there are lots of things going wrong in other schools.' Ethan tried to think of an explanation. 'Perhaps he just wanted Ms Mountain to organize the Mega Conference. So he could hypnotize the other Heads, like Mr Ramsey and Miss Davidson.'

Lizzie frowned. 'Why wouldn't he do anything at Hazelbrook?'

'Maybe . . . because of us? We beat him, didn't we? And made him look stupid.'

'You really think he's scared of a crowd of kids?' Lizzie laughed and shook her head.

'Not *scared*. But he might want to avoid us. Maybe—' Ethan's brain made a huge, frightening leap. '*Maybe that's what this island trip is about.*'

Lizzie looked baffled. 'What do you mean?'

'Maybe the trip was meant to get us out of the way.' Ethan was working it out as he spoke. You and me. And Blake and Tyler and Angelika. There are five people going on the trip, right? And there are five of *us*.'

'*Six*,' Lizzie said.

Ethan shook his head impatiently. 'The Headmaster wouldn't count Robo. He thinks there are five of us, and he meant us all to go away for a week. With Ms Mountain. Can't you see what he's planning? *That's when he's going to take over Hazelbrook!* Only his plan hasn't worked. Angelika and I will still be here.'

Lizzie bit her lip. 'So . . . should the rest of us stay too?'

Saying that must have been a struggle. Ethan knew how much she wanted to go to the island. 'No, you must still go,' he said. 'We don't want the Headmaster to know we've guessed his plan. Angelika and I will be here to keep watch. If anything strange starts happening, we'll let you know. And you can tell Ms Mountain she's got to come back.'

Lizzie nodded. 'We need to tell the others then. So they know what's going on.'

'Not yet,' Ethan said. 'We've still got a few days left before you go off to the island. Let me see what I can find out before that.'

He spent the whole weekend hunting for information about New World. There was lots on the internet now—because New World was taking over more and more schools.

The interviews with children and teachers all said the same things:

Our school is efficiently organized now . . . Learning targets are being met exactly on time . . . All the pupils are perfectly behaved . . .

So what was it *really* like in a New World school?

Ethan phoned Sam, to try and find out.

'How are things?' he said. 'Is the school different without Mr Ramsey?'

'Our school is very well organized,' Sam said in a cool voice. 'Learning targets are being met and all the pupils behave perfectly.'

Ethan shivered. It was horrible hearing Sam talk like that. 'So what about your band?'

'Music has its place in the curriculum,' Sam said smoothly. 'It is not necessary to extend that beyond school hours.'

'*What?* Don't you want to play outside school? Just for fun?'

'We should focus on things which are useful to society,' Sam said. 'Now I must go and do my Physics homework. Goodbye, Ethan.' He rang off, without waiting for Ethan to say anything else.

Ethan gave himself a few minutes to calm down. Then he phoned Jatinder and asked the same question.

'Is the school different without Mr Ramsey?'

'Our school is very well organized,' Jatinder's voice was stiff and distant. 'Learning targets are being met and all the pupils behave perfectly.'

'What about IT?' said Ethan.

'I am proud to be learning skills that will make me a useful member of society. Business and industry need a good supply of competent IT professionals.'

'But are you *enjoying* it now?'

'Computers should not be used for amusement,' Jatinder said. 'Information Technology is a serious part of the economy.'

Ethan wanted to shout *Stop it!* He wanted to go round to Jatinder's house—and Sam's too—and yell at them until they started talking like themselves again. But he knew it wouldn't work. They wouldn't change until the Headmaster was stopped.

He spent Sunday evening writing down everything he knew. About the DVD and the mysterious voice. And New World taking over one school after another. And the way Sam and Jatinder were talking. And Ms Mountain and the trip to the island.

It all added up. He was sure the Headmaster had a plan for Hazelbrook too. And Ethan and his friends— the people who might interfere—were all supposed to be far away on the island. Ethan was sure he was right.

Except . . .

Somewhere, at the back of his mind, there was a fact that didn't quite fit. What was it? He went over everything again—the Arts Explosion, New World, the DVD—but he couldn't work out what it was. And there was no more time to think. He needed to show the others what he'd written, so they could talk about it on Monday morning, before Lizzie and the others left for the island.

He added one last line to what he'd written:

The Headmaster is DEFINITELY planning something. We need to talk.

Then he sent it off and went to bed.

The island trip was supposed to be leaving at lunchtime. Ethan set off early on Monday morning, so they all could talk before school started.

But he hadn't counted on a change of plan.

As he cycled round the last corner, he saw a minibus outside the school gates, just pulling away from the kerb. *Oh no! They can't be going already—*

But they were. Angelika was standing outside the school with her mother, waving goodbye, and as the minibus came towards him, he saw Lizzie and Tyler inside, with Blake in front of them.

He waved as hard as he could, but Tyler and Blake were talking and they didn't see him. Lizzie was the only one who waved back, and that was just for a second. Then the minibus disappeared round the corner and they'd gone.

He *had* to talk to them. Pulling out his phone, he called Lizzie, as fast as he could.

Angelika started walking up the road towards him, as the phone rang and rang against his ear. She was shaking her head, and when she reached him she took something out of her pocket.

'*No* chance,' she said. She was holding two phones. Tyler's, in its robot case, and Lizzie's little silver one.

Ethan stared. 'Why have you got those?'

'They had to leave them behind.' Angelika pulled a face. 'Ms Mountain said it at the last minute, after Lizzie and Tyler's dad had gone off to work. There's no signal on the island, and she wants the trip to be a *phone-free space*.'

'You mean . . . they're out of contact?' Ethan said slowly.

Angelika nodded. 'Except for the satphone.'

'The what?'

'Ms Mountain's hired one, so she can send pictures back to the school.'

No other phones? Ethan didn't like the sound of that. 'Do you know the satphone number?'

Angelika shook her head. 'My mum's got it, but she won't tell me. It's just for emergencies, she says.'

So it was just the two of them, then. On their own against the Headmaster. Ethan took a long, deep breath. Then he looked at Angelika.

'OK,' he said. 'There's something I need to tell you . . .'

19

THE ISLAND

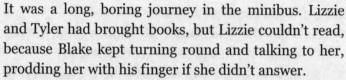

It was a long, boring journey in the minibus. Lizzie and Tyler had brought books, but Lizzie couldn't read, because Blake kept turning round and talking to her, prodding her with his finger if she didn't answer.

'. . . We must be going to stop soon . . . It's going to be very late when we get there . . . Look, is that a Lamborghini? . . .' In the end, Lizzie gave up on her book and let him talk.

He was very excited. 'There's going to be rock climbing! And kayaking! And Ms Mountain says we'll have a special Expedition Leader . . .'

Lizzie stared out of the window, only half-listening as they travelled up one motorway after another. M1, M6, M74 . . . Mr Wasu and Ms Mountain sat at the front, talking to the driver, and there were three or four stops at service stations, but only for half an hour, so they could eat their snacks and packed lunches.

It seemed to take hours, but at last they were off the motorways and onto smaller and smaller roads . . .

It was almost dark when the minibus finally stopped. Lizzie looked out of the window. They were in a little grey town, parked in a small, empty car park. On one side of the car park was a short row of shops. All closed. On the other side was the sea.

Mr Wasu looked out of the window. 'This is the place?' he said, sounding surprised.

Ms Mountain nodded briskly. 'This is where we get out of the minibus.' She looked round and raised her voice. 'Collect up your bags, everyone. Make sure you don't leave anything behind.'

Blake jumped up straight away and grabbed his rucksack, pushing through the door ahead of everyone else. But Tyler had fallen asleep. Lizzie shook his shoulder.

'Wake up, Ty. We're here.'

Tyler blinked and opened his eyes. 'On the island?'

'No, silly. We have to go on a boat. Come on.' Lizzie picked up his bag, and her own, and looked back at Robo, who was strapped into the seat behind them. How was she going to manage him, and two bags, and a sleepy Tyler?

'Want some help?' said a voice from the back.

It was Conan O'Dell, the fifth person on the trip. He was a tall, skinny boy and he took Lizzie and Tyler's bags as well as his own and nodded at Robo. 'Want me to carry him too?'

'It's OK. I can manage. Thanks.' Lizzie pulled Tyler onto his feet and gave him a push. 'Go on. Follow Conan and I'll bring Robo.' She nudged Tyler out of the bus and lifted Robo down behind him.

The moment they were all out, the minibus driver

nodded and started the engine. A couple of seconds later, he'd gone, and they were standing in the rain, all on their own in the wet car park. Mr Wasu muttered something to Ms Mountain. Lizzie didn't catch the words, but she could see he looked worried.

'There's no problem,' Ms Mountain said loudly. 'The boat will be here in ten minutes.'

It felt like weeks to Lizzie. Tyler kept whining, because he was cold, and Blake kept pointing out to sea and saying, 'Is that a boat?'

It would be getting dark when they got to the island. How would they pitch their tents? And what about food? They hadn't had anything to eat for hours. Lizzie was very anxious—and she thought Mr Wasu was too, because he kept frowning and whispering to Ms Mountain.

But Ms Mountain just smiled and waved her hand. 'The boat will be here soon. No problem.'

They'd been waiting almost half an hour when a small boat finally came chugging round the headland on their right and drew in next to the carpark wall. A small, grey-haired man looked up at them.

'You'll not be going to Murdoch's Island tonight?' he said.

'Of course we are,' Ms Mountain said briskly. 'Quickly, everyone. Into the boat.'

The old man shook his head at her. 'It'll be thick dark by the time you're landed. Would you not do better to wait till morning?'

'No need for that,' Ms Mountain said brightly. 'This

trip is all about adventure. Arriving in the dark will be part of the excitement.'

Lizzie could see the boatman didn't like it, but Ms Mountain ignored his face and shepherded them all on board. 'We're off!' she said, as the boat turned towards the sea.

Blake let out a loud whoop. 'Island, here we come!'

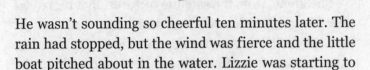

He wasn't sounding so cheerful ten minutes later. The rain had stopped, but the wind was fierce and the little boat pitched about in the water. Lizzie was starting to feel seasick, for the first time in her life.

'I have your tents,' the boatman was saying to Ms Mountain. 'But I'm guessing you'll spend the night in the bothy and put them up tomorrow morning?'

'Of course not!' Ms Mountain looked amazed. 'We'll be getting our camp together tonight. Before we go to sleep.'

Mr Wasu opened his mouth. And shut it again.

The boatman frowned. 'You're all experienced campers?' he said hopefully.

'Oh no.' Ms Mountain gave him a cheerful grin. 'This will be my first time under canvas. *Very* exciting.' She grinned at Mr Wasu. 'Yours too?'

Mr Wasu swallowed nervously. 'I went camping once, when I was in the Cubs.'

'Hmm.' The boatman looked past him. 'What about the rest of you? Any campers on board?'

Blake and Tyler shook their heads. So did Lizzie—

trying not to panic. But Conan nodded. 'I've been camping all my life.'

The boatman beckoned to him and the two of them talked quietly for ten minutes, as the island got closer and closer. Lizzie recognized it straight away. It was too dark to make out the cliffs that fell vertically towards the water, but the shape of the mountain was still clear against the darkening sky.

She knew, from the satellite pictures, that there was only one place to land—a little bay where a stream cut through the cliffs. As they approached it, the boatman steered towards a small wooden jetty on the left of the bay. When he had moored the boat, he opened a locker under his seat and took out four tent bags.

'You'll be needing my help,' he said. It wasn't a question. 'The boy Conan and I will take charge of two tents each and the rest of you will help when you're asked. In the meantime—' he nodded at their backpacks and cases '—you can carry up your luggage.'

He gave Robo a disapproving look and turned on a big, powerful torch. Then he started unloading the bags onto the jetty.

They couldn't have done it without Conan and the boatman. They hauled the tent bags up the steep track from the bay and along a narrow path, with the boatman shining the light ahead of them. Conan went last, because he had a big torch too.

They stopped beside a small stone building with a

single window and a battered wooden door.

'Here's the bothy,' said the boatman. 'And this ground here is for your camp. This side of the mountain, you'll be sheltered from the wind and the worst of the rain.' He set his torch down on a rock beside the bothy and nodded at Conan. 'Let's get them up.'

There were two single-person tents—one for Ms Mountain and one for Mr Wasu—and a couple of two-person tents for everyone else. *Good*, thought Lizzie. *That means I'm sharing with Tyler*. He might be frightened in the dark.

It was almost half an hour by the time the tents were pitched and all their gear was stowed inside. The moment it was done, Ms Mountain beamed at the boatman. 'Thank you for your help, Mr Fraser. We'll see you on Friday.'

The boatman hesitated, as if he wasn't happy about leaving them. 'Is there not another person coming?'

'Our Expedition Leader arrives tomorrow,' Ms Mountain said cheerfully. 'Don't worry about us. We'll be in good hands—and we'll sleep well tonight!'

The boatman shook everyone's hand and headed back down the path. As soon as he had gone, Ms Mountain handed out protein bars.

'Eat these, as fast as you can, and then into your sleeping bags,' she said.

Lizzie shepherded Tyler into the tent. It was a squash, because he insisted on having Robo in with them, but at least they were dry and out of the wind. They crawled into their sleeping bags without undressing, and Tyler fell asleep instantly.

The last thing Lizzie heard, before she fell asleep too, was Ms Mountain's voice, booming across the campsite.

'Sleep well, everyone. The Expedition Leader comes tomorrow—and you're going rock climbing!'

20

THE HELICOPTER

Ethan wasn't expecting any news from the island. But when he and Angelika walked into school the next morning, there was a huge crowd round the big screen outside the hall. They were staring up at a picture.

'It's the island!' Angelika said. 'Ms Mountain must have sent it.'

Ethan nodded. It had to be the camp where the others were staying. Four very small tents were pitched next to a little stone building covered in moss. The ground round the tents was littered with boulders and the tent flaps were blowing open. It all looked horribly uncomfortable.

On the other side of the building, was a small black helicopter.

Our Expedition Leader has arrived said the message across the bottom of the photo.

Angelika shivered. 'I'm glad I'm not there,' she muttered. 'Thank goodness Ms Mountain asked me to give up—' She stopped and put a hand over her mouth.

'What?' Ethan said sharply. 'What did she ask you to give up?'

Angelika glanced at all the other people round them and shook her head. 'I promised not to tell,' she muttered.

Ethan went cold. *That* was what he'd forgotten, when he was working out the Headmaster's plan. It was nothing to do with the Arts Explosion. Or New World. He'd forgotten the weird conversation with Ms Mountain, when she'd asked him to give up his chance of going to the island, to help Lizzie.

Why would she do that, if the Headmaster wanted them all out of the way?

He looked at Angelika. 'We have to talk. Where no one can hear us.'

'We can't do that now. It's registration in a moment.'

'At break then. Behind the gym. OK?'

Angelika shrugged, looking puzzled. 'OK. If you like.'

The first lesson was Maths, one of Ethan's favourite subjects, but he couldn't concentrate on it. He was furious with himself. *You fool*, he kept thinking. *You idiot!! You complete and UTTER MORON!!!* He'd been so sure he was right that he hadn't seen the gaping hole in his neat little theory about the Headmaster.

He'd got everything wrong.

The moment the bell went for break, he was out of the classroom and out of the building. He thought he might have to wait for Angelika, but she was only a couple of seconds behind him.

'OK,' she said. 'You've been looking like a ghost all morning. What's wrong?'

Ethan took a long breath. 'After the first round of the competition, Ms Mountain called you into her office, didn't she? She said Blake was in danger of not getting picked for the island trip and she asked you to give up your own chance of going, and help him instead. And she told you to keep it a secret. Right?'

Angelika stared. 'How did you know all that?'

'Because the same thing happened to me. Ms Mountain asked me to give up *my* chance of going, so I could help Lizzie. And she told *me* to keep it secret too. Don't you see what that means?'

Angelika chewed her lip, working it out. 'But I thought you said the Headmaster wanted us *all* on the island? To get us out of the way.'

'I did,' Ethan said miserably. 'But I think I got it wrong. It looks as though we've been split up. Deliberately. Whatever the Headmaster's planning, he doesn't want us together.'

Angelika went pale. 'You mean . . . he might be planning something on the island?'

Ethan nodded. 'That black helicopter—does it remind you of anything?'

'It's like the New World car, isn't it?' Angelika shivered. 'Do you think Simon Weatherby is the Expedition Leader?'

'I think he might be,' Ethan said slowly. 'But if so, what has the Headmaster sent him to do? We don't know. And we can't find out—because there's no phone contact.'

For a second, the two of them stared at each other. Then Angelika snapped her fingers. 'What about the DVD? That might tell us what he's up to. Maybe it's still in Ms Mountain's office.'

'Won't the office be locked?'

'Yes—but my mum has the key.' Angelika thought for a moment. 'It's no good trying to explain all this to her. Not until we've got some proof. But I know where she keeps her keys. *And* the code for the school burglar alarm.'

'You mean . . . we're going to break in?'

'Yes!' Angelika said. 'Let's do it tonight, after the cleaners have gone. I have Youth Club on Tuesday evenings, so Mum won't wonder where I am.'

Ethan nodded. 'OK. I'll tell Auntie Beryl I'm going for a cycle ride. What time?'

'Eight o'clock. At the main entrance. Right?'

'Right!'

21

THE PRECIPICE

At that very moment, Lizzie was standing at the bottom of a cliff, staring up at the sheer rock face.

Halfway up, in his ordinary trainers, a battered old harness, and a helmet that didn't fit properly, Blake was hanging onto two protruding pieces of rock. One of his feet was jammed on to a tiny little ledge and the other one was waving around in the air.

'I can't find it!' he was yelling. 'I can't find the foothold!'

Ms Mountain was up at the top of the precipice, where Blake's safety line was fixed round a huge boulder. She leaned over the edge and shouted down. 'Stay calm. And try a bit higher.'

Blake's left leg flailed around in the air, scraping against the cliff face. Conan was standing next to Lizzie, and she heard him mutter, 'Where's the Expedition Leader? He should be here.'

None of them had seen the Leader so far. His helicopter had landed very early in the morning. They'd heard it coming, but by the time they had scrambled out of their sleeping bags he was already inside the bothy. Ms Mountain and Mr Wasu had both been in to see him, but he hadn't set foot outside it. *Must be doing his paperwork*, Conan had said scornfully.

Lizzie looked up at Blake and then glanced at the bothy. The door was firmly shut. 'Do you think Blake's really in trouble?' she whispered.

Conan looked up at the cliff and pulled a face. Lizzie thought he was going to say something, but he didn't. Instead, he turned away and marched off to the bothy. Lizzie heard him banging on the door.

Tyler crept up beside her. 'Is Blake OK?' he whispered nervously.

Lizzie looked back at the cliff. Ms Mountain had disappeared from the edge and now Mr Wasu was looking down.

'Right, Blake,' he said, in a steady voice. 'Do exactly what I say and you'll be fine. Stop wriggling about and let your right leg hang straight down. Done that? OK, now move it ten centimetres to the right. Then up about twenty centimetres . . .'

For a second, Lizzie thought Blake was panicking too much to obey the instructions. Then his right foot edged outwards and upwards, one centimetre at a time, until it lodged in a crack so small that Lizzie could hardly see it.

'Good!' Mr Wasu called down. 'Nearly there. Now move your left hand . . .'

Blake reached up for the next handhold—and his left foot slipped off its ledge. That jerked his body and his right foot slipped too. For one terrible second, his whole weight was hanging on the rope.

Then he grabbed a lower piece of rock and his left

foot scrabbled its way into a hole. Steadying himself, he leaned forward against the cliff.

'Slowly now. Slowly.' Mr Wasu's voice was shaking. 'Find the other foothold.'

Blake's foot scrabbled against the rock, missed the ledge, and then found it again.

'Steady now.' Mr Wasu's face was pale. 'Take a break before you move again.'

Lizzie could hardly breathe for the next five minutes. Very slowly, Blake inched up the cliff, stopping to rest after each movement. When he finally reached the top, Ms Mountain and Mr Wasu caught hold of him and pulled him up onto the grass. Lizzie could see him lying there, trying to get his breath back.

She was concentrating so hard she didn't notice Conan coming back from the bothy. When she looked round, he was standing next to her.

'Did you see the Expedition Leader?' she whispered. 'What did he say?'

Conan looked back at her. 'Everything is proceeding according to plan,' he said, in a flat, unemotional voice.

Lizzie was puzzled. Was he joking? 'Did you tell him Blake was in danger?'

'Ms Mountain is in charge,' Conan said, still in the same mechanical voice. 'She has done a full risk assessment.'

Lizzie looked back at the cliff. Tyler was standing at the bottom, gazing up at Mr Wasu and Ms Mountain. They were facing each other and it looked as though they were arguing.

Ms Mountain flapped her hand, dismissing whatever it was that Mr Wasu had said. Then she bent down to Blake, who was still lying on the ground, and took off his helmet and the harness he was wearing.

'Here you are, Tyler!' she called. 'Your turn next! Put these on.' And she threw them down to him.

No! Lizzie thought. *NO!* She wasn't going to let that happen, however many risk assessments there were. Racing forward, she caught hold of Tyler's arm. 'Don't do it,' she whispered.

Tyler was very pale. 'I'm not scared,' he said.

'Of course you aren't. It's just . . . I'm going up to talk to Ms Mountain. OK?' Lizzie raced up the zigzag path at the side of the cliff. By the time she reached the top, she was completely out of breath. Before she could speak, Ms Mountain started yelling again.

'Come on, Tyler! Show Blake you're a better climber than he is. Put the harness on and I'll throw you the rope.'

'No!' Lizzie struggled to get the words out. 'No . . . Ms Mountain, it's . . . too dangerous! You mustn't—'

You mustn't make Tyler do it, she was going to say. But before she could get the words out, Ms Mountain picked up the rope, ready to throw the end down to Tyler.

'You need to clip this on to the harness,' she shouted.

Lizzie took one look at the rope—and went cold. 'No!' She was so choked she could hardly get the words out. 'No—look—'

Near the top, where it had rubbed against the cliff,

the rope had almost worn through. It could snap at any moment. If that had happened when Blake's feet slipped, he would have fallen twenty metres, crashing down to the ground.

And that could happen to Tyler.

Lizzie turned and shouted down to him. 'No, Ty! NO! You mustn't start climbing!'

She saw his head tilt back as he looked up. And, at the same moment, she heard a gasp from behind her. It was Ms Mountain. She was staring down at the frayed rope in her hand, blinking as though she had just woken up.

She took a step forward and bellowed down at Tyler and Conan. 'Sorry, boys! No more climbing today. Get your cagoules and we'll go for a hike round the island instead.'

As they turned and ran back to the tents, she looked down at the rope again and Lizzie heard her muttering to herself.

'I don't get it. No one should be climbing with a rope like this.'

22

NIGHT RAID

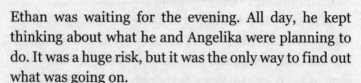

Ethan was waiting for the evening. All day, he kept thinking about what he and Angelika were planning to do. It was a huge risk, but it was the only way to find out what was going on.

As soon as he got home, he started on his homework. He kept going until teatime and then went back to it afterwards, but he couldn't concentrate. He kept making mistakes and checking the time every couple of minutes.

At a quarter to eight, he stood up and stretched. 'Finished!' he said loudly. 'I think I'll just go for a quick cycle ride. I need some exercise.'

Auntie Beryl looked at her watch. 'It'll be getting dark quite soon. Are your bike lights working?'

'They're fine. I changed the batteries when I got home from school.' Good thing he'd thought of that.

Auntie Beryl gave him a grudging nod. 'All right then. But be back in half an hour.'

Ethan nodded. Crossing his fingers behind his back, because he wasn't sure how long it would take.

When he reached the school gates, they were already

unlocked. He slipped through, pushing them almost shut behind him, so no one would notice they were open. Angelika's bike was lying in the bushes beside the gate. He hid his own bike there too and crept up to the main entrance.

Angelika was standing in a shadowy corner. When she saw him, she nodded. 'Ready?'

Ethan nodded back and she gave him a grin and tapped in the entrance code. As soon as the door opened, the alarm started up and Angelika raced into the office at top speed, with Ethan behind her. Within five seconds, the alarm was off and everything was quiet. She and Ethan crouched behind the counter, until they were sure no one was coming, and then Angelika took a torch out of her pocket.

'Can't risk the lights,' she hissed.

Jerking her head towards the door, she crawled out of the office, with Ethan close behind her. When they were out in the corridor, she stood up and produced a bunch of keys.

'Here we go,' she whispered. 'I'll look on the shelves. You check her desk. And be quick. We need to be out of here fast.'

There were five keys on the ring and she had to try three before she found the right one. As they crept into the office, Ethan looked at the light switch and decided they couldn't risk it, even with the blinds closed. He'd have to use the light on his phone. As Angelika made for the shelves, he tiptoed across to Ms Mountain's desk.

There was no sign of the DVD in the clutter on top of

the desk. If it was there, it must be in one of the drawers. He opened the bottom one and started searching.

Ms Mountain kept a weird collection of things in there. A chocolate bar. A packet of balloons. Three thin books of poetry, a games console, and a ball of purple string.

But no DVD. And it wasn't in the middle drawer either.

He could hear Angelika working her way along the shelves, muttering to herself. 'Complete Shakespeare . . . Keep Fit in Fifty Minutes a Week . . . Rapping for Beginners . . .' It didn't sound as though she was having any more luck than he was.

Then Ethan opened the top drawer—and there it was, lying on top of a big brown envelope. A DVD in a plain brown sleeve, with a label that said exactly what he'd guessed. *To my successor*.

'Got it!' he whispered.

Angelika turned round and grinned. 'Fantastic. There's loads of DVDs over here. Let's put one of those in the drawer, so no one guesses there's anything missing.' She took a box off the shelf. 'This is a set of Christmas film. No one's going to be needing those for a while.'

Ethan slipped one of the Christmas discs into the brown sleeve and dropped the real one in his pocket. He was just about to put the substitute into the drawer when he noticed something.

The brown envelope that had been underneath was labelled *Island Adventure*.

What was inside? It wasn't sealed, so he opened it and took out the papers inside. The top sheet was headed **Island Adventure: Risk Assessment**. It looked like a standard form, with some of the columns filled in:

Activity	Rock climbing	Kayaking	Mountaineering???
Potential Hazards	Rope breaking	capsizing	Rocks
People at Risk	Blake Vinney	Tyler Warren	Lizzie Warren
Safety Measures			

Angelika frowned. 'I don't understand. Why are there different people at risk? Aren't they all doing every activity? And what about the safety measures?'

Ethan stared down at the paper, with a horrible idea growing in his mind. He was just about to tell Angelika what he was thinking when she switched off her torch and nudged him sharply, pointing out of the window.

'Quick!' she muttered. 'We need to get out!'

There was a small light moving round at the main gate.

Ethan slid the paper back into its envelope and dropped it into the drawer, with the substituted DVD on top. Before he had even closed the drawer, Angelika was out in the corridor. Ethan ran to join her and she locked the door behind him.

'This way!' she hissed. 'Can't risk the front door.'

She raced down the corridor that led to the gyms, with Ethan close behind her. Slipping through the door at the far end, they shut it quietly behind them and stood listening for a moment. Someone was walking up the path to the main entrance.

The footsteps reached the door, hesitated and then started moving round the outside of the building, coming towards them. Angelika tugged at Ethan's sleeve and they crept round the back of the school, as fast as they could, being careful to stay on the grass.

They were almost round to the front when the feet behind them started running. Pulling up their hoods, they raced for the gate and dragged their bikes out of the bushes.

'You go first,' Ethan panted. 'I'll distract him. Meet at my place, OK?'

Angelika nodded and cycled off at top speed. She was still just in sight when the man appeared round the side of the building. Ethan gave a loud shout, to distract him.

'Wait for me!' he called—looking in the opposite direction, as if Angelika was there.

Then he cycled off that way. No one on foot was going to catch him and there was a little alley just ahead. If he turned down that, no car would catch him either.

When he reached the alley, he glanced back quickly, to see if he was being chased. He saw a man step through the school gates, turning to look down the road towards him. In the glare of the security light, the man's hair was unmistakably red.

Had he seen him? Ethan wasn't going to stay and find out. He pedalled off down the alley, as fast as he could, with his brain buzzing.

What was Simon Weatherby doing at Hazelbrook? And if he wasn't on the island—who was?

23

KAYAKS IN THE DARK

As Ethan and Angelika raced off, Lizzie was sitting by a campfire, eating a baked potato. Everyone was there—except the Expedition Leader. He was still inside the bothy. Mr Wasu kept glancing at the door, looking puzzled, as though he was expecting him to appear. But the door didn't open.

Tyler didn't care. He was chattering away as he mashed butter into his potato. 'Wasn't it great hiking round the island? I can't wait to go up the mountain!'

But Lizzie kept looking at the door too. She couldn't stop thinking about what she'd seen at the top of the cliff. That rope. Why hadn't Ms Mountain and Mr Wasu seen how dangerous it was? And what kind of Expedition Leader would let that happen?

She'd tried talking to Conan about the rope, but he said things like, 'Everything is in order' and 'A risk assessment has been done'.

And Blake wouldn't listen either. He was embarrassed about being bad at rock climbing. 'It's all fine,' he said gruffly. 'I'm not looking for excuses.'

That only left Tyler. And she had no intention of telling him what she'd seen. She didn't want to give him nightmares. So she sat quietly, eating her baked

potato; thinking, *Maybe it's best not to make a fuss.*
They weren't going to be doing any more rock climbing.

She thought they would be sent to bed when they'd
finished their potatoes. But she was wrong. As Tyler
pushed the last piece of crunchy skin into his mouth,
Ms Mountain looked round at them all.

'Right!' she said. 'Are you ready for a *real* adventure?'

Mr Wasu blinked. He obviously hadn't been
expecting that.

'We're going kayaking!' Ms Mountain said.

'Kayaking?' Tyler was so excited he started bouncing
up and down. 'Can Robo come too?'

Ms Mountain beamed at him. 'Of course. Get him
out of the tent and let's go!'

Tyler jumped up and shot across to the tent. 'We're
going in a *boat*, Robo,' Lizzie heard him whisper. That
sounded like a really bad idea to her, but she didn't
have a chance to argue. Blake and Conan were already
on their feet and Ms Mountain was beckoning them all
to the path behind the bothy.

Lizzie looked at the bothy door, expecting it to
open. But it didn't. Where was the Expedition Leader?
Shouldn't he be going with them?

There was no time for questions. Ms Mountain was
leading them down the path to the little jetty where they
had landed when they arrived. Tyler had to carry Robo
down, because the slope was too steep for his wheels,
and Lizzie heard him whispering all the way.

'You're going to love it, Robo. You can show
everyone how clever you are.'

When they reached the jetty, they found five small blue kayaks tied up next to a pile of paddles. Tyler squealed with excitement.

'Look, Robo!' he said. 'There's one for you!'

Blake gave a snort of laughter. 'That's *dumb*. Robo can't paddle a kayak.'

'Yes, he can,' Tyler said. 'I just need to program his arms to do the right movements. Ethan showed me how. Look, it's brilliant.' He stood with his eyes closed for a moment, moving his own arms to work out what they did when he paddled. Then he pressed some buttons on Robo's control panel and stood in front of him, making the movements again.

For a second, nothing happened. Then a blue light flashed and Robo began to move his own arms in the same way as Tyler, copying his exact movements.

'You see?' Tyler said. 'If I tell him to remember that, he'll add it to his menu.' He tapped the control panel. Then, when the robot's arms stopped moving, he picked him up and slipped him into one of the kayaks, closing his metal fingers round the paddle. 'Robo's ready!' he said. 'And so am I.'

Ms Mountain grinned. 'Then off you go!'

'Wait a moment!' Lizzie said.

But it was too late. Robo and Tyler were both paddling away across the dark water—without life jackets.

Ms Mountain turned to Blake. 'Now you,' she said.

'No! Me!' Lizzie didn't wait for Ms Mountain to agree. She grabbed a paddle and a kayak and set off after Tyler, as fast as she could.

It was ridiculous. It was *dangerous*! They shouldn't be out on the water on their own, with no instructor and no life jackets. It wasn't like being on a lake. This was the sea and there could be rocks and currents and—

Lizzie didn't want to count the dangers. She just wanted to catch up with Tyler and make him come back. He wasn't used to paddling and she could see he was already getting tired. He kept stopping for a second or two, to rest his arms.

But Robo didn't need to rest, his arms kept moving, round and round, forwards and backwards, on and on and on, like—like a machine.

Lizzie couldn't waste time worrying about him. All her energy was focused on catching up with Tyler. She had almost reached him when he stopped paddling and gave a loud yell.

'No, Robo! Stop!'

Lizzie looked past Tyler—and saw the huge, jagged pillar of rock in Robo's way. It stuck up straight out of the water, like a dagger, and Robo was heading straight for it.

There was no time to do anything. Robo was too far ahead. As they watched, his kayak drove straight into the rock and tipped up, sending Robo tumbling into the water.

'Noooo!' wailed Tyler.

He started paddling again, so fast that Lizzie could hardly keep up with him. But it was no use. By the time they reached the rock, the kayak was floating upside down and they could see Robo sprawled out below them, way down on the sea bed.

For one terrible moment, Lizzie thought Tyler was going to crawl out of his kayak and dive down to try and rescue his robot. But even he could see it was impossible. He sat in his kayak with tears streaming down his face.

'Robo's gone,' he sobbed. 'He's *gone*.'

24

OUTRAGE!

Ethan took the DVD out of his pocket. He and Angelika were sitting side by side in front of his laptop, sharing the headphones.

'Ready?' he said.

Angelika nodded, and Ethan pushed the DVD into the laptop. For a split second, there was silence. Then an icy voice said, 'Welcome to Hazelbrook,'—and there he was.

The Headmaster.

Even though Ethan was expecting it, he froze with shock for a moment. The Headmaster's green eyes stared out of the screen, like huge, gleaming pools of water. Deep, deep pools . . .

'Look into my eyes,' murmured the Headmaster's voice. 'Look deeper . . .'

Ethan stared, feeling himself being drawn towards them. Closer and closer . . .

'No!' Angelika said fiercely. She lowered the lid of the laptop, until the picture was hidden. 'Ethan, you idiot! You looked at him!'

Stupid! Ethan couldn't believe he'd been so close to getting hypnotized. He gave Angelika a quick, grateful grin and then closed his eyes, concentrating on what he was hearing.

For a few moments more, the Headmaster's voice went on murmuring softly, saying words like *tired* and *drowsy* and *sleep*. Ethan shivered. If Angelika hadn't half-closed the lid when she did—if he'd still been looking at the screen—he would have been in the Headmaster's power by now.

But he and Angelika were still wide awake when the Headmaster's voice changed. Suddenly, it wasn't soothing any more. It was cold and business-like.

'Open your eyes,' it said briskly. 'Look at me. Here are your instructions.'

It didn't take them long to play the whole DVD. It only lasted for a quarter of an hour. But when it finished, they couldn't speak for a moment. They sat staring at the half-closed laptop, with terrible words going round and round in their minds.

... *important to separate the troublemakers* ...

... *select the most dangerous activities* ...

... *arrange a fatal accident* ...

'I got it wrong,' Ethan said. It was like a nightmare. 'The Headmaster's not planning to do anything *here*. It's all going to happen on the island. And Lizzie and the others—' He was too choked to finish.

'We have to call the police,' Angelika said.

'What can we tell them?' Ethan shook his head. 'If we say Ms Mountain's hypnotized, they won't believe us. Unless we show them the video. And if we do that—'

'—they'll be hypnotized too.' Angelika nodded. 'But we've got to do *something*. The Headmaster's up there on the island, Ethan. And we're the only people who know what he's planning.'

Ethan's mind raced round and round in circles, desperately trying to work something out. He was still thinking when Auntie Beryl shouted from the sitting room.

'Ethan! Angelika! Come and look at this!'

'We're—er—just doing something,' Ethan called back.

'Well, stop it! Come here! It's outrageous!'

'Better go,' Angelika whispered, and they went into the sitting room.

Auntie Beryl was staring at her tablet. When she saw Ethan and Angelika, she picked it up and waved it at them. 'Look at these pictures! They're up on the school website.'

Ethan and Angelika went and looked over her shoulder. 'We've seen that one,' Ethan said. 'It's the camp on the island. Where Lizzie and the others have gone.'

Auntie Beryl swiped sideways. 'Well, how about *this* one?'

Ethan looked—and his mouth dropped open. It was a picture of Blake, halfway up a cliff, in a helmet that didn't fit. He was hanging from a rope, with his legs flailing in the air, and he looked terrified. But Ms Mountain was grinning down from the top of the cliff, as if it was all a joke.

'And *this*?' Auntie Beryl said, in a terrible voice.

She swiped again—and there was a big, jagged rock sticking up out of a stretch of dark water. On the left of the rock, a small blue kayak floated upside down, as if it had capsized. On the right, in another kayak, was—Tyler. He was staring at the upside-down boat with his mouth wide open, as if he was shouting. And there were tears running down his face.

He looked devastated.

'No!' Angelika whispered.

Auntie Beryl rolled her eyes. 'These things are happening on a school trip? It's out of control!'

Ethan was too horrified to speak. He stared at the picture, thinking, *Who was in the other canoe?*

Auntie Beryl's phone pinged. And then pinged again. And again. She didn't bother to look at the messages. 'That's how I knew about the pictures,' she said. 'Everyone's talking about them. Ms Mountain has to go!'

'We should call the police!' Angelika said fiercely.

Ethan's heart jumped. Was this their chance? Had the Headmaster made a mistake? For a couple of seconds, he thought their problem was solved.

Then Auntie Beryl pulled a disapproving face. 'The school can do without *that* kind of publicity,' she said. 'We don't want Hazelbrook splashed all over the national news.'

'But we can't just leave them on the island,' Angelika said. 'Not if it's *dangerous*.'

Auntie Beryl patted her hand. 'Don't worry, dear. The governors have found a better way than calling the police. New World will sort it out for us.'

New World! Ethan and Angelika looked at each other. 'What are they going to do?' Ethan said.

'They're going to rescue our children,' Auntie Beryl said soothingly. 'That nice Mr Weatherby is going to take a minibus up there—with your mother, Angelika. They'll bring all the children back, without any fuss. They're going off first thing in the morning. Isn't that kind?'

It wasn't *kind*. Ethan was sure of that. But did it mean the danger was over? That Simon Weatherby would bring everyone back safe and sound? For a second, he almost believed that was the answer.

Then he remembered the Headmaster's voice ordering Ms Mountain to *arrange a fatal accident*. He glanced sideways, at Angelika, and saw that she was remembering it too.

'Let's go and finish off on the computer,' he said brightly.

As soon as they were on their own, he switched off his laptop and took a long breath. 'We need to let the others know they're in danger. Your mum's going up there with Simon Weatherby. You need to tell her what we've found out.'

'I'll *try*,' Angelika said doubtfully. 'But suppose she doesn't believe me?'

'Maybe she'll take a letter for Lizzie. That would be better than nothing.'

Angelika nodded slowly. 'All right. I'll talk to her as soon as I get home. I'll let you know what she says.'

Ethan was almost ready for bed when Angelika's message came through. He put down his toothbrush and read it straight away.

Tried telling Mum. She said don't be ridiculous. Won't take a letter either. Says New World is sorting everything and DON'T INTERFERE.

But they *had* to interfere—to stop something dreadful happening. If Angelika's mother wouldn't help them, there was only one other way. Ethan reread the message, to make sure it really was as hopeless as he thought. Then he sent his answer.

Then I have to be on the minibus. What time are they leaving?

He thought Angelika would tell him it was impossible. But she didn't. She answered straight away.

He's picking Mum up at 6 a.m. Leave your bike in the back alley and I'll hide it. BE CAREFUL.

So she agreed with him. There was no other way to save their friends. He had to get himself onto the minibus—somehow.

Ethan finished brushing his teeth and set his alarm for 5 a.m. With any luck, he could be out of the house before Auntie Beryl woke up . . .

25

CONFRONTING
THE LEADER

It was hard to get Tyler back to the jetty. Lizzie managed it, paddling her own kayak and pushing his ahead of her, but when they were there, he didn't want to go back up to the tents.

'We can't leave Robo,' he wailed.

'We can't do anything tonight,' Lizzie said. 'We'll come back tomorrow.'

Scowling at Ms Mountain and Mr Wasu, she chivvied Tyler away from the jetty and up the path. She had no idea what they were going to do in the morning, or how Robo could possibly be rescued, but she knew *exactly* what she was going to do next. As soon as Tyler was safely asleep.

She made him get into his sleeping bag and sat beside him until his eyes closed and he stopped sobbing. Then she crawled out of the tent and looked round. Blake and Conan were in their own tent, talking quietly, and Ms Mountain and Mr Wasu were sitting by the campfire, staring into the embers.

Quick, Lizzie thought. *Before they notice me.* She was going to shout at the Expedition Leader. What did he think he was doing? Why didn't he come out of the bothy and *lead*? She marched across and knocked on the battered black door of the bothy. Then she flung it open, without waiting for an answer.

It was dark in there, but she could see a tall figure standing on the far side. He was staring through the window that looked out over the sea.

'What are you doing, stuck away in here?' she said, in a tight, angry voice. 'If you don't come out and start *leading*, someone's going to get hurt.'

'That would never do, would it?' murmured the dark figure. He turned towards her, but his face was still in shadow. All Lizzie could see was a dark shape, outlined against the pale shape of the window. He reached out an arm, pointing at the table beside the door. 'Turn on the lamp,' he said.

Lizzie felt around for the lamp. When she clicked the switch, the bothy was filled with a thin, chilly light. She turned to look back at the Expedition Leader—

—and there he was. The Headmaster. Staring straight at her.

'Good evening, Lizzie Warren,' he said.

There was a split second when Lizzie could have turned away, or covered her eyes, but for a moment she was too shocked to react. And then it was too late. She was gazing into the Headmaster's pale, cold eyes, and his voice was speaking very softly, creeping into her mind.

'You must be very tired after all the excitement . . . so tired you can't keep your eyes open . . . so tired that you're drifting away . . . drifting . . .'

The next thing she knew, Lizzie was walking out of the bothy, closing the door quietly behind her. Ms Mountain and Mr Wasu had disappeared, and the campfire was just a pile of ashes. It looked as though everyone else was fast asleep.

I must go to sleep too, she found herself thinking. *I need to set out early tomorrow. I must go to sleep now . . .*

She crawled into the tent, without waking Tyler, and wriggled into her sleeping bag. As she closed her eyes, the same thoughts were running round in her mind, again and again. *I must go to sleep now . . . I need to set out early tomorrow . . . I must go to sleep . . .*

When she woke up, it was still dark. She had no idea what time it was, but before she had time to think she found herself crawling out of her sleeping bag and fumbling around to find her shoes. *I must go*, she was thinking. *It's time to go.*

As she reached out to open the door of the tent, Tyler moaned in his sleep. She didn't want to leave him. He was going to be very unhappy when he woke up and remembered about Robo. She wanted to stay and look after him, but she couldn't ignore the voice in her head.

I must go . . . It's time to go . . .

She fumbled in her backpack, to find her little torch and her notebook. By the light of the torch, she scribbled a quick message to Tyler.

I have gone up the mountain. Ms Martin told me I had to go ahead, to reconnoitre the track for everyone else.

Reading it through, she thought, muzzily, *There's something wrong with that*. But she couldn't work out what it was. And the voice in her head was getting louder and louder.

It's time to go . . .

Ripping out the page, she laid it down very carefully, beside Tyler's head, where he couldn't possibly miss it when he woke up. Then she dropped the torch into her backpack, crawled out of the tent and stood, looking up at the mountain.

It loomed ahead of her in the darkness, with the sky just beginning to grow light behind it. Yesterday, she'd seen a broad track leading up the main slope, but now the whole mountain was a single black shape.

Shouldering her backpack, she crept past the other tents and started trudging towards it.

26

STOWAWAY

Ethan managed to leave without waking Auntie Beryl. He left a note on the kitchen table.

Gone off early, to meet Angelika. We're doing a project together. Might need to meet after school too.

With any luck, she wouldn't start worrying until he'd had a chance to talk to Lizzie. He couldn't think beyond that.

And it wouldn't happen unless he reached the island. As he pedalled through the dark streets, he kept trying to work out what to do at the end of the journey. Even if he did manage to sneak onto the minibus, he wouldn't be on the island when that part of the journey ended. He would still have to get across to the island. How was he going to do that?

He reached Angelika's house without finding an answer. It was still only a quarter to six and there was no sign of the minibus, so he pushed his bike down the alley at the side of the house. Angelika must have been watching for him, because the back gate opened straight away.

'Quick! Put it in the shed!' she hissed.

Ethan pushed the bike in and Angelika hid it under a bundle of plastic netting.

'I've made a kind of plan,' she whispered. 'When Simon Weatherby gets here, he's got to leave the minibus, to knock on our door. That's your chance. Go round to the far side of the minibus—where he can't see you—and *be ready*.'

That was all she had time to say. The next moment, they heard the sound of an engine coming up the road. Angelika shot back into the house and Ethan crept back to the top of the alley and waited in the shadows, with his heart thumping.

There was no mistaking the minibus. When it pulled across the road, it stopped under the street light outside Angelika's house, and Ethan could see the New World logo gleaming golden against its shiny black side. The door banged as Simon Weatherby got out and walked up the path towards the front door. As he rang the bell, Ethan shot out of the alley and crept round to the far side of the minibus.

Everything happened very quickly. Angelika opened the front door and Ethan heard her call out to her mother.

'Your coat must be somewhere. I'll take your bag while you look.'

She raced down the path, carrying a small red bag, and opened the back doors of the minibus, waving at Ethan to tell him to jump in.

'Quick!' she muttered. 'They won't see you if you're

on the floor, between the seats.'

She shut the doors and stood by the side of the minibus, blocking the window to hide Ethan as he clambered over the back row of seats. He lay down on the floor, between that row and the next one, curling up to make sure that his feet were out of sight.

It was incredibly uncomfortable, but he didn't dare to wriggle. He could hear feet coming towards the minibus. A moment later, Simon Weatherby climbed into the driver's seat and started the engine. And he heard Angelika's mother saying goodbye.

'Be a good girl, Angie. Dad's coming round at seven, to take you to school, and you're going home with him till I get back.'

There was a mumble from Angelika and then the front passenger door opened and closed again.

'Sorry to keep you waiting, Mr Weatherby,' Angelika's mother said. 'I can't *think* how my coat got into the utility room.'

Ethan smiled to himself. He thought he knew how that had happened.

It was his last smile for a long time. The next moment, the minibus pulled away from the kerb and he started the most uncomfortable journey of his life.

As Ethan travelled north, curled up in the back of the minibus, Lizzie was walking along the wide, stony track that led up the mountain in the centre of the island.

When she set out, it was still not properly light

and she had to use her torch to find the beginning of the track. But once she was there, a voice seemed to whisper inside her head.

Don't need the torch now. Turn it off. Don't need the torch . . .

She flicked the switch and plodded on automatically in the dim grey light, climbing slowly upwards. Not thinking. Not wondering why she was out on her own, in the half-dark. Just putting one foot in front of the other. Left, right, left, right, left . . .

As it climbed, the path curved round the side of the mountain. Soon, the tents and the bothy were out of sight and Lizzie found herself walking up a narrow valley with a little stream running down the centre.

At the top of the valley, the track curved left, starting a long, slow zigzag to the summit. Lizzie turned to follow it, but, as she took the first step, she heard the whispering voice again.

Turn right at the top of the valley. Follow the little track. Find the cave . . .

Mechanically, she turned round and looked the other way. Until then, she hadn't even noticed the faint, narrow track on the slope to the right. Now she saw it and her feet moved by themselves, leaving the wide, clear track she'd been following until then. The temperature was dropping and she had started to shiver, but she hardly noticed as she started edging along the tiny path, holding on to bushes, to make sure she didn't lose her footing on the slope.

As she went, mist started coming down on the

mountain. At first there were only a few wisps, floating ahead, but soon it was all around her. After a few minutes, she couldn't see anything except the tiny stretch of path in front of her. Normally, she would have understood what a dangerous thing she was doing. But now there was nothing in her mind except the tiny, whispering voice.

Follow the little track. Find the cave.

Left, right, left right, left . . .

27

LOST!

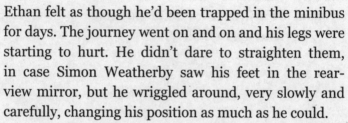

Ethan felt as though he'd been trapped in the minibus for days. The journey went on and on and his legs were starting to hurt. He didn't dare to straighten them, in case Simon Weatherby saw his feet in the rear-view mirror, but he wriggled around, very slowly and carefully, changing his position as much as he could.

That wasn't the thing that bothered him most. The question that kept going round and round in his head was, *What happens at the end of the journey?* When the minibus finally stopped, his problems wouldn't be over. He would still have to get across the sea.

How was he going to do that?

He lay on the floor, worrying and wriggling—as much as he dared—trying to make a plan. Was there a ferry that went to the island? Could he swim across? What about trying to borrow a boat?

If only he knew what it was going to be like when he got there.

In the end, all his plans were useless. He didn't have a chance to choose what happened to him.

When the minibus finally stopped, Simon Weatherby

said, 'We're here,' and switched off the engine.

For a second, there was complete silence and, in that silence, a message came in on Ethan's phone. He had set it to vibrate, but even the vibration made a tiny sound.

'What the—?' Simon Weatherby said. He looked over his shoulder and then jumped out of the minibus and slid the side door open. 'Is there someone there?'

There was no point in trying to hide any more. Ethan crawled out from behind the seats and stood up, very shakily.

Angelika's mother looked round and gasped. 'Ethan!'

Simon Weatherby gave her a sharp look. 'You know this boy?'

'He's one of our students—a friend of my daughter's.' Mrs Maron shook her head at Ethan. 'What are you doing here?'

Ethan thought quickly. He couldn't tell her the truth. If he tried, Simon Weatherby would know they'd discovered the Headmaster's plan. He hung his head and tried to look pathetic. 'I wanted to see the island. It looks so lovely in all the pictures.'

'You stupid boy!' Mrs Maron frowned. 'What are we going to do with you?' She glanced at Simon Weatherby, as though she expected him to give her an answer.

His face was blank. 'I have no instructions about that,' he said.

'Well, we can't leave him here, all on his own. He'll have to come with us.' Mrs Maron sighed impatiently.

'Where's this boat you've arranged? We have to get across to the island as fast as we can.'

Problem solved. Ethan looked down at his feet, so they wouldn't see how relieved he was. Now he knew how he was getting to the island. Once he was there, he could warn Lizzie and the others, and they would be facing the Headmaster *together*. Ready to defeat him again!

Simon Weatherby was on his phone, talking to the boatman. When he finished, he jerked his head at Ethan. 'Out!' he said. 'The boat's just coming.'

Ethan scrambled out. He could hear the sea, lapping against the low wall on one side of the car park, and he turned to look at it. Would he be able to see the island?

He couldn't see anything at all. There was a thick, white mist lying over the sea, blotting out the whole view.

When the boat arrived, the boatman was looking out to sea and shaking his head. 'You'd do better to wait,' he said to Simon Weatherby. 'It won't be easy, making a landing in this.'

'We must leave at once,' Simon Weatherby said stiffly.

Mrs Maron nodded. 'Please,' she said. 'We think the children are in danger. If they get injured—'

'They'll not be doing anything in this weather,' the boatman said. 'Their leaders will have them telling stories round the campfire. If they have any sense.'

'That's just it. We don't think—' Mrs Maron stopped and bit her lip. 'Please take us. We have to get there before something terrible happens.'

The boatman looked at her face. Then up at the sky. Then out to sea. Then he gave a grudging nod. 'We'll need to take it slowly, mind. And I'm not promising anything.'

They scrambled down into the boat and it headed out into the blank, white mist.

High up on the mountain, Lizzie was staring out into the same thick mist. It had come down while she was still walking across the slope, and she'd hardly been able to see her feet on the faint, narrow path.

When she had finally reached the cave, she'd crawled in, straight away, and huddled against its rocky wall, trembling and shaken. The cave was just a narrow crack, only big enough for one person, but at least she was safe there. She wouldn't lose her footing and go slithering down the mountainside.

She kept trying to calm down, but every time she tried to think sensibly the little voice in her mind started whispering again.

When you reach the cave, you will be too frightened to move. You will be too frightened to speak. You will do nothing until you hear my voice again . . .

Nothing.

Not even when she heard someone calling her name, far away on the main track.

'Lizzie! Where are you? Can you hear me, Lizzie?'

You will be too frightened to speak . . .

'Lizzie!'

The voice went on calling her name for a long time. For hours. Huddled inside the cave, Lizzie heard it moving slowly up the mountain. Then it came down again, still calling. But she couldn't move. She couldn't make a sound. It wasn't the right voice.

You will do nothing until you hear my voice again . . .

And then there was no more calling. She was alone in the cold mist.

28

TO THE RESCUE

By the time the boat finally reached the island, Ethan was shivering. He only had his ordinary jacket and the mist was very cold. The boatman tied up at a little wooden jetty and pointed at a stony path ahead of them.

'You'll find their camp up there, by the bothy. Will you be wanting me to come with you?'

'That won't be necessary,' Simon Weatherby said crisply. 'Please wait here. We may be some time. The boy will stay on the boat.'

No! Ethan thought. But he didn't need to say it. The boatman agreed with him.

'I'll not be looking after any boys,' he said crisply. 'That's your job. I hope you do it better than the last lot I brought over.'

'We've come to fetch them home,' Angelika's mother said. 'If you could just wait—'

The boatman shook his head. 'Sitting around in the mist is no part of my job. I'll be back to collect you at nine o'clock tomorrow morning. If it's safe to land.'

He waited just long enough for them to climb ashore and then untied the boat and set off back to the mainland. Simon Weatherby shouldered his bag and looked at Mrs Maron.

'Don't worry,' he said. 'New World is here to solve all your school's problems.'

Sounds like a slogan, Ethan thought. But he didn't say anything. He just trudged up the path behind the other two, wondering what they would find when they reached the camp.

Hoping they weren't too late.

When they reached the top of the path, they could see a little stone building ahead of them, with a group of tents beyond it.

'There they are!' Angelika's mother said. She sounded relieved. 'The boatman was right. They're sitting round a campfire. They're safe!'

For a moment, Ethan thought she was right. But the group round the campfire didn't look very cheerful. He started counting them.

'Where's Lizzie?' he said. And his heart thumped. *That upside-down kayak . . .*

At the sound of his voice, everyone in the group looked round. As soon as Tyler saw who it was who had spoken, he jumped up and raced towards Ethan.

'Lizzie's up the mountain!' he said. 'She's up there, all on her own!'

'What?' Angelika's mother looked horrified. 'How on earth—?'

'She went off very early,' Tyler said. He looked desperate. 'She just left a note and *went*.'

Ms Mountain came hurrying across to meet them. 'Mr Wasu went to look for her,' she said. She looked desperately worried. 'Straight away, as soon as Tyler showed us the note. He's been gone for hours. I don't know what else to do. Someone has to stay here with the other children. And there's no way of contacting Mr Wasu.'

'What about the Expedition Leader?' said Angelika's mother.

An odd change came over Ms Mountain's face. She blinked once and then looked round calmly. 'I am the Head of Hazelbrook,' she said. 'I take full responsibility.'

Angelika's mother looked puzzled. 'But—'

She didn't get to the end of her sentence. Before she could finish, a shout went up from the campfire.

'There's Mr Wasu!' It was Blake. Jumping to his feet, he pointed into the mist.

'Where?' That was Conan's voice.

'Quick!' Tyler caught hold of Ethan's hand and dragged him towards the fire.

All Ethan could see was a tall figure coming out of the mist. They were almost at the campfire before he could be sure it was Mr Wasu.

Ms Mountain came racing past them. 'Where's Lizzie?' she shouted. 'Is she injured?'

Mr Wasu stumbled towards them and slumped down onto one of the log benches beside the fire, shaking his head miserably. He looked utterly exhausted. 'I couldn't find her,' he said. His voice was so hoarse it was almost a croak. 'I went all the way up the track—right to the very top of the mountain. And I shouted her name all the way up and all the way down. But there wasn't any answer. If only I'd been able to see a bit more—'

He stopped, as if the words were choking him. Ms Mountain put a hand on his shoulder. 'You did what you could,' she said. She squatted down beside him and went on talking, very quietly.

'He hasn't found Lizzie!' Tyler was almost in tears. 'She's still out there, Ethan. All on her own! We have to go and look for her!'

'What can we do in this mist?' Ethan said.

Blake was sitting with his back to them. At the sound of Ethan's voice, he looked round in amazement. 'How did *you* get here?'

For a second, Ethan couldn't think how to explain without being overheard by Simon Weatherby. Then he started shivering again. 'I came across in the boat,' he said quickly. 'And I'm *freezing*. Could you lend me a jacket, or something?'

'Got a couple of hoodies in the tent,' Blake said. 'Come on.'

They both crawled into the tent and Ethan put his mouth close to Blake's ear and whispered, 'You're all in danger. The Headmaster's *here*, not at Hazelbrook. He's planned some kind of terrible accident.'

Blake's eyes opened very wide. '*He's* the Expedition Leader?' he whispered back.

Ethan nodded. Then he raised his voice. 'That hoodie's huge. Haven't you got a smaller one?'

Blake got the message. 'Here!' He pulled a thick hoodie out of his bag and pushed it at Ethan. 'Try this then—Shortie.'

With a quick grin, Ethan took off his jacket. As he

pulled on the hoodie, he heard a little noise outside. It wasn't coming from the campfire. It was over the other way, by the bothy.

The sound of a door opening, very quietly. And then closing again.

Blake frowned. He'd heard it too. 'What's that?' he whispered.

They crawled out of the tent and looked towards the bothy. Beyond the building, they could see a tall, dark figure moving briskly towards the mountain, growing blurred and indistinct as it disappeared into the mist.

Ethan shivered. And not because he was cold. 'It's him,' he whispered. 'He's going after Lizzie.'

'We have to follow him,' Blake said.

Ethan glanced over his shoulder, towards the campfire. No one was looking their way. Everyone was firing questions at Mr Wasu, trying to work out why he hadn't seen Lizzie on the mountain. 'They won't notice if we go now. Come on—before they stop us.'

Blake nodded and they edged backwards, step by step, away from the tents and the campfire. Making for the path the Headmaster was following.

29

IN THE MIST

Lizzie was cold and hungry. Inside the cave, she was sheltered from the wind, but she had been out on the mountain for almost twelve hours, with nothing to eat. All she had was the bottle of water in her backpack, and that was empty now. Her mouth was very dry and she was struggling to breathe.

She knew it wasn't sensible to stay in the cave, that she wouldn't survive unless she struggled back along the narrow path and down the mountain. But every time she tried to move, her legs refused to carry her. There was nothing she could do about it.

You will be too frightened to move . . . You will do nothing until you hear my voice again . . .

But she wasn't going to give in. She kept trying to crawl out of the cave, over and over again. And she kept leaning forward, listening for a sound—any sound—that might mean someone was out there on the track. They wouldn't just leave her. People were bound to come looking. And when they did, she would make a sound, somehow. She *had* to.

It was her only hope.

Ethan and Blake were creeping along behind the Headmaster. They were well up the mountain now, where they wouldn't be heard from the campsite, and the Headmaster was striding up the track ahead of them. They were just managing to keep him in sight through the mist.

Then suddenly—he wasn't there. The track took a turn to the left and when they reached the bend they could see it stretching ahead of them. Completely empty.

Blake peered into the mist, frowning and shaking his head. Then he turned towards Ethan and opened his mouth.

No! They mustn't make any noise! Ethan shook his head fiercely, putting a finger to his lips. Blake held up a hand, to show he understood. Then he leaned forward suddenly, peering over Ethan's shoulder.

What had he seen? Ethan spun round. For a second, he couldn't see anything except the stony track behind them and the thick white mist. Then there was a movement, away to one side, and he saw what Blake had seen.

The Headmaster had left the main track. He was walking along a narrow path that curved round the mountainside, and he was almost out of sight.

'Quick!' Blake whispered. 'We mustn't lose him. Lizzie might be along there!' Hurrying past Ethan, he stepped onto the narrow path and started creeping along behind the Headmaster.

Be careful! Ethan thought. He followed Blake, as

fast as he could, but it was difficult to move quietly. The path was narrow and uneven and there was a steep slope on the left-hand side, with lots of loose rocks, ready to fall if anyone touched them.

The slope was worn away where streams had cut into it and the path curved in and out, following the shape of the ground. Twice they lost sight of the Headmaster, when he went round a spur ahead of them. Ethan could tell that Blake was getting anxious, because he started to hurry.

And that made him careless.

The Headmaster vanished for a third time, hidden by the shape of the ground, and Blake began to jog. *Careful!* Ethan thought. But it was too late for that. Blake caught his foot on a rough patch in the path and reached out a hand, to steady himself against the slope.

He brushed against a loose stone and it fell out of the slope, rolled across the path and went tumbling down the side of the mountain.

Blake froze. Ethan froze. For a moment they didn't even breathe. But there was no sound from ahead of them and no tall, dark figure came striding back round the spur.

Ethan moved forward, very carefully, and touched Blake's shoulder. *I think it's OK*, he mouthed. Together, they moved slowly forward, round the spur.

And came face to face with the Headmaster.

He was standing waiting for them, so close that they could see him clearly, in spite of the mist. His pale face was tight with rage.

'So—you are meddling again!' he hissed. 'You will regret your clumsy interference in my plans!'

'We won't regret anything!' Blake shouted. 'We know what you're doing and we're going to stop you.'

'Stupid boy!' The Headmaster's hand went up to his dark glasses. 'You think you can resist?' Suddenly the glasses were off, and they were looking straight into his icy, glittering eyes.

No! Ethan thought. *No!* He heard Blake gasp beside him. But it was too late. Neither of them could look away from those cold, compelling eyes. Ethan felt himself being drawn in, deeper and deeper, sinking down and down and down . . .

30

UNTIL YOU HEAR MY VOICE

'So—you are meddling again!'

The sound was just loud enough to reach Lizzie, crouched in her cave on the other side of the stream. She blinked and lifted her head. Somewhere in her brain, she heard a little whisper, fading away.

You will do nothing . . . until you hear my voice again . . .

Where was she? What was she doing, in this tiny, dark space with water trickling down beside her? Why did she feel as though she'd just woken up? For a second, she was completely confused.

The voice spoke again. 'You will regret your clumsy interference in my plans!' It sounded like the Headmaster. But why was he here? Unless . . .

Had they been wrong about his plans?

Then there was a shout that Lizzie recognized for certain.

'We won't regret anything! We know what you're doing and we're going to stop you.'

That was Blake! What was he doing there? Crawling forward, very slowly and carefully, Lizzie put her head out of the cave and looked across the stream.

There was the Headmaster, standing with his back

to her. Just beyond him were Blake—and *Ethan*. And the Headmaster was reaching up to take off his glasses. He was speaking more softly now and Lizzie couldn't hear the words. But she didn't need to. She knew what they were.

Look into my eyes . . .

The Headmaster was hypnotizing Blake and Ethan. Standing on the side of the mountain—on a narrow path where they needed to concentrate to keep their balance—he was *hypnotizing* them. Lizzie didn't know what he was planning, but it was certainly dangerous. He had to be stopped.

Very quietly, she crawled ahead, until she was right out of the cave. Then she stood up and looked across the stream again. Blake and Ethan were staring ahead, with their eyes wide open and their faces blank. They were completely motionless. She knew they wouldn't see her now, whatever she did. And the Headmaster still had his back to her.

When he spoke to the boys again, his voice was clear and crisp. 'Here are your instructions. When I clap my hands, you will turn right and walk three steps forwards . . .'

But that would take them over the edge of the path! They would go crashing down the side of the mountain!

Lizzie watched in horror as the Headmaster raised his hands in the air and clapped once. The sound echoed off the rocks and Ethan and Blake turned towards the sheer drop on their right.

'NO!' Lizzie yelled. But the boys' faces were

completely blank. She knew they couldn't hear her. Flinging herself forward, she exploded across the stream, charging straight at the Headmaster.

The boys took a step forward, towards the sheer drop in front of them—and the Headmaster turned towards Lizzie, taken completely by surprise.

She only meant to push him out of the way, but as she reached him she caught her foot in a pothole and fell forward, crashing into him with her whole weight. He lurched sideways, clutching at the rock beside him, but it came away in his hands. Before he could recover, he fell sideways off the path.

Lizzie caught hold of Ethan and Blake, hauling them back from the edge. They stood side by side, listening to the Headmaster yelling with fury as he slid down the mountain and disappeared into a clump of trees.

And then there was silence.

For second, Lizzie couldn't move. She couldn't speak. She just stared down the slope, struggling for breath.

Ethan blinked, as if he had just woken up. 'Where's the Headmaster? He was just here—'

'He was telling you to walk off the path,' Lizzie said unsteadily. 'You would have fallen straight down there. So I pushed him out of the way. But I didn't mean—' She stopped, feeling sick, and pointed down at the steep, rocky slope.

'He's right down *there*? In the trees?' Blake's mouth fell open and he leaned forward, staring. 'Do you think he's all right?'

'I don't know,' Lizzie said miserably. 'Perhaps he's broken his leg. Or . . . something worse. What are we going to do? We can't just leave him there. Not if he's injured.'

They looked at each other. And then down at the trees. Lizzie was shaking and she could see the boys felt the same as she did. But . . . what else could they do?

'*He* would have left *us* down there,' Blake muttered.

Ethan shook his head. 'Lizzie's right. We've got go down and look for him. But it's too steep to try here. Let's go back to the main track first and walk down to the trees.'

Lizzie nodded and they started walking back along the narrow path, being careful not to stumble. When they reached the main track, they ran down to the start of the trees and peered into the wood. But they couldn't see very far. The ground under the trees was thick with bushes and brambles.

'We'll have to go in,' Lizzie muttered. 'Let's spread out. But don't lose sight of each other. And if you see him—'

Ethan nodded. 'Shout straight away. And DON'T LOOK AT HIM!'

They stepped off the path and began to work their way into the forest. It was almost impossible to stay in touch with each other. Lizzie had to change course almost at once, to avoid a thicket of holly bushes. When she looked round, the boys were nowhere in sight.

She turned back, towards where she'd last seen

Ethan—and something tugged at her jacket. For a second, she was too terrified to move. Then she looked down and saw it was a bramble. With her heart thudding against her ribs, she unhooked it and crept on into the trees.

They hunted for almost half an hour, but they didn't see the Headmaster. And there was no sign of a body. All they found was a place where the brambles were flattened and branches had snapped off the trees. After half an hour, they decided they would have to give up.

'We'll have to tell Ms Mountain,' Lizzie said, as they struggled back towards the track. 'And Simon Weatherby. They'll have to come and search. We can't—'

Before she could finish, Blake caught at her arm. 'What's that noise?'

There was a strange rushing noise coming from the foot of the mountain, getting stronger every second. Blake put his head down and charged through the tangle ahead, clambering out on to the track. As he turned to look down towards the bothy, his mouth fell open and he pointed up at the sky.

'Look!' he shouted. '*Look!*'

31

NOT BEATEN YET?

Ethan and Lizzie battered their way through the last few brambles and hurried out onto the track. The moment they were clear of the trees, they saw why Blake had shouted.

The Expedition Leader's black helicopter—the *Headmaster's* black helicopter—was rising high into the air above the bothy, turning towards the mainland.

'It's him!' Lizzie said. 'It has to be.'

Ethan couldn't see who was in the helicopter, but he knew they had to find out. Pulling out his phone, he zoomed in, as much as he could, and started taking photos, focussing on the helicopter's windows. He kept on until it set off across the water, dwindling into the distance. Then they all huddled round the phone, peering at the pictures.

Lizzie frowned. 'It looks as though there are *two* people in there. Who's the other one?'

'I don't know,' Ethan said grimly. 'But we have to find out. Come on!'

And they all started running down the track.

Even before they reached the camp, they could hear

Ms Mountain shouting.

'It's *appalling*! How *could* they go off like that? It's *CRIMINAL*!'

When they came round the last bend, they saw her outside her tent. She already had a pack on her back and she was bending down to lace up her climbing boots—still shouting.

'I can't believe I asked him to lead this expedition! How could he go off and ABANDON CHILDREN like that?'

'Hey!' Ethan called, waving both arms in the air. 'Hey, Ms Mountain! We're here!'

Ms Mountain straightened up—and Ethan had never seen anyone look so relieved. She came charging up the path, without bothering to tie her laces.

'I was coming to find you!' she shouted. 'What happened?'

Everyone else was close behind her. Tyler flung himself at Lizzie, hugging her as hard as he could.

'You should never have been out there on your own.' Ms Mountain shook her head. 'I thought the Expedition Leader was looking for you—but he just flew off! With that man from New World!' Her eyes blazed. 'They just *left* –with you three lost on the mountain, and the night coming on.'

'We saw them go,' Blake said. 'Ethan's got pictures of the helicopter.'

Ethan held his phone under Ms Mountain's nose and she gave him an approving nod. 'Good boy. That's *evidence*. We have to make sure everyone knows what

New World is *really* like.'

Ethan grinned back at her. He was just going to put the phone away when he saw there was an unopened message. How had it had reached him, with no signal on the island?

For a second, he was baffled. Then he remembered the message that had given him away, when he was in the minibus. Things had happened so fast since then that he'd forgotten all about it. He flicked it open, not expecting anything important—and gasped.

'What's the matter?' Lizzie said.

It was a message from Angelika.

Protest meeting about island photos. Tomorrow evening at 7 p.m. Parents are calling for New World to take over.

Ms Mountain's mouth dropped open. 'New World—at Hazelbrook? Never! We have to get back for that meeting!' She looked across at the sea. 'But how—?'

'The boatman's coming back tomorrow morning,' Ethan said. 'At nine o'clock—if the weather's OK.'

'Then we'd better be ready.' Ms Mountain looked round briskly. 'We'll pack up our bags tonight and the tents tomorrow morning. And I'll call through on the satphone, to make sure there's a minibus waiting.'

Everyone was nodding. Except Tyler.

'But Robo—' He sounded as if he was going to burst into tears.

Ms Mountain gave him a long, careful look. Then she said. 'You're in charge of packing up, Conan. I've got something else to do before we can leave.' She smiled at

Tyler and ran off towards the campsite.

Angelika's mother watched her go. 'She's a *great* Head,' she said sadly. 'It's a tragedy she's going to resign.'

'RESIGN?' Blake looked horrified. 'She can't do that!'

'She thinks she *has* to,' Mr Wasu said. 'Because she put you all in danger.'

'Well, we're not going to let it happen!' Blake said. He beckoned to Ethan and Lizzie and Tyler. 'Start thinking! We have to find a way to stop her.'

By the time it was dark, they had the beginnings of a plan—which was good, because they had no time to think after that. The next day started with a rough boat trip, followed by a hectic journey down the motorway. Their minibus reached the school car park two minutes before the meeting was due to start.

Angelika came running out to meet them. 'The hall's packed,' she said. 'And all the parents are really angry. They're saying terrible things about you, Ms Mountain.'

Ms Mountain climbed out of the minibus and stood up, very straight. 'I'll just have to go and face them,' she said. And she walked into the school.

'Quick!' Lizzie grabbed Tyler's hand. 'We mustn't give her a chance to say she's resigning.' She ran after Ms Mountain, with the others close behind her.

'It's—those photos—from the island,' Angelika panted. 'They're so terrible—'

'Don't worry.' Ethan grinned at her. 'We've got a plan.'

They were right behind Ms Mountain as she walked into the hall. When the parents saw her, there was a huge roar of rage. For the first time ever, Lizzie and Ethan saw Ms Mountain hesitate.

That gave Blake the chance he needed. He ran down the hall and jumped on to the platform, bellowing at the top of his voice.

'SO—DID YOU LIKE MY TRICK PHOTOS?'

That stopped the noise. Every parent in the hall stared up at him. For a second, nobody spoke. Then his father shouted up at him.

'What are you talking about? You were nearly killed. We saw the picture.'

Blake shook his head, with a cheeky grin. 'Haven't you heard of fake news? I *tricked* you! I was only a metre above the ground, really. And that picture of Tyler in the kayak? More fake news! You can't blame Ms Mountain for those photos.'

Because she was hypnotized when she sent them, Ethan thought. But it was no use trying to explain *that* to the parents. Much better to remind them what a great Head Ms Mountain was.

And there wasn't much time left. Ms Mountain was climbing onto the stage now and the parents had started muttering. Any minute now, she'd start talking about resigning. Ethan nodded to Lizzie and they hurried round the side of the hall, to the computer.

As they reached it, Ms Mountain turned to face the

parents and there was an angry shout from a man in the front row.

'You're finished! What this school needs is *New World*!'

Until that moment, Ms Mountain looked apologetic and unhappy. But when she heard the words *New World*, she fired up, whirling round to face down the hall.

'NO ONE needs New World!' she bellowed. 'They're not fit to be in charge of any school!'

'She's right!' Lizzie shouted from beside the computer.

'Look at these!' yelled Ethan. And he flashed up one of his photos of the New World helicopter onto the screen behind Ms Mountain.

She wasn't expecting it, but she reacted straight away. 'You know who's in that helicopter?' she shouted. 'Simon Weatherby! The man you want to put in charge of Hazelbrook! As soon as we had a problem, he *ran away*—taking the Expedition Leader with him. That's how much he cares about your children!'

The parents were quiet now, but some of them were still muttering. Lizzie leaned closer to Ethan. 'Ready with the video?' she muttered.

He nodded and Lizzie waved to Tyler on the other side of the hall. *Time to go!*

Tyler ran up onto the stage. 'New World ran out on us!' he shouted. 'But Ms Mountain wouldn't leave *anyone* behind. Look!'

He waved at the screen and the helicopter picture

disappeared. In its place, was a jagged rock pillar, sticking straight up out of the sea. As they watched, a massive, scarlet figure hauled itself up the pillar. At the top, it stood straight for a moment and then leapt into the air and shot down like a rocket, diving straight into the water.

'That's Ms Mountain!' Tyler yelled. 'That's how she rescued Robo! SHE'S A HERO!'

For a second, there was a startled silence. Then the hall exploded into laughter and cheering. Blake's father leapt to his feet, waving his arms in the air.

'Ms Mountain for ever!' he yelled.

Everyone started yelling the same thing. All Ms Mountain could do was stare round the hall, with her mouth wide open. Looking gobsmacked.

Ethan grinned at Lizzie. 'We've done it!' he said. 'She won't be *able* to resign now. They won't let her.'

Lizzie grinned back. He was right. They'd beaten New World and saved the school. Everything was going to be OK.

But she couldn't help wondering where the Headmaster had gone . . .

CAN YOU RESIST . . . ?

YOU'LL NEVER BELIEVE WHO HE'S AFTER THIS TIME ...

THE DEMON HEADMASTER AND THE PRIME MINISTER'S BRAIN

GILLIAN CROSS

IT'S THE LATEST CRAZE ... BUT BEWARE!

THE REVENGE OF THE DEMON HEADMASTER

GILLIAN CROSS

HIS MOST TERRIFYING PLAN SO FAR ...

THE DEMON HEADMASTER TAKES OVER

GILLIAN CROSS

WHO IS HIDING BEHIND THE MASK ...

FACING THE DEMON HEADMASTER

GILLIAN CROSS

TERRENCE HARDIMAN   TESSA PEAKE-JONES

THE DEMON HEADMASTER
THE COMPLETE SERIES

THE CLASSIC CBBC CHILDREN'S TV SERIES
INSPIRED BY THE BOOKS

THE DEMON HEADMASTER COMPLETE SERIES
AVAILABLE TO BUY ON DVD AT WWW.SIMPLYHE.COM

Ready for more great stories?

Try one of these ...

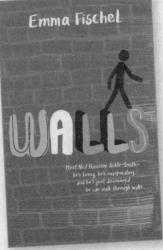